Let it Melt

by

Margot Johnson

Merilee Tours, Book 2

Let it Melt

Cover Art by *The Wild Rose Press, Inc.*

The Wild Rose Press, Inc.
PO Box 708
Adams Basin, NY 14410-0708
Visit us at www.thewildrosepress.com

Publishing History
First Edition, 2022
Trade Paperback ISBN 978-1-5092-4216-0
Digital ISBN 978-1-5092-4215-3

Published in the United States of America

"But…" She hadn't danced a polka since before her divorce. She breathed the warm air, circulating faint scents of cinnamon and vanilla from the bakery. Remembering the giddy exhilaration of keeping pace with accordion sounds, she wavered.

Just as the playlist broke into one of the most famous polka songs, Jack clasped her hand and swung onto the dance floor.

The organ-like sound overtook her reticence, and she followed his lead. Hopping and spinning, she matched her rhythm to the music and synched with his bounces and swoops. His hand was so hot on her back it nearly sizzled. She floated in dizzying circles faster and faster, until she laughed and begged Jack to slow. She hadn't whirled this light and carefree in years. Finally, the music hit its final note. Puffing, she glanced at Jack, and her breath caught in her throat.

He stared deep into her eyes, blinked, and touched the tip of her nose with a gentle finger. "Well done."

Elation and confusion waltzed in her stomach, and her pulse raced. "I had fun. Thanks for the invitation." Shaken, she broke away and collapsed into a chair against a wall. For most of the evening, she had merely endured Jack's company. Now, why did she struggle to remove herself from his arms?

Praise for Margot Johnson

Dedication

For my mom and in memory of my dad, Diane & Ian Bickle. I couldn't wish for more loving and devoted parents.

Acknowledgments

Many thanks once again to my dedicated editor, Leanne Morgena, for going above and beyond to make sure this story of Merilee's Sweetheart Tour was ready in time for Valentine's Day. You catch everything I miss and make my stories better.

To my valentine, Rick ~ you are my dream date for a Sweetheart Tour! Thank you for always being there. Hugs to our big, blended, and extended family ~ you warm my heart with support and fun. Also part of the family, our old golden retriever, Sophie, keeps me company while I write and is the inspiration for the dogs in my books.

Finally, thank you to everyone who told me LET IT SNOWBALL gave you a warm, festive feeling and to everyone who's on board for Merilee's latest tour.

I love to hear comments and reviews from readers! Please contact me and sign up for news at margotjohnson.ca. You'll also find me on Facebook: Margot Johnson Author and Twitter: @AuthorMargot

Prologue

Hurrying through Saturday errands, Jill Meyers paused, sniffed the clean, winter air, and scanned a large, pink poster in the window of Omar's Foods in Goldview, Saskatchewan.

Love is Wined & Dined!
Cuddle up on a Sweetheart Tour
Gourmet meal...Love songs...
Red roses...Chocolate kisses!
February 1-14 Book now!
1-800-FUN-TOUR merilee@funtour.com

She rolled her eyes and hustled along the street. The event might appeal to the happy couples in town, but it sure wasn't designed for a mature divorcee without a partner. Deep loneliness squeezed her heart. A romantic bus tour was the last place she'd belong.

Chapter 1

SASK radio announcer: "I asked my buddy if he had a date for Valentine's Day. He said, 'Yes. It's February fourteenth.'"

****

In the school parking lot, Jill Meyers idled her car to warm the engine for the short trip home. In the small town of Goldview in the Canadian prairies, everything she needed was close. Normally, she'd walk to and from school, but today's frigid temperature chased her to her car. The heater whined, and she turned up the radio volume to more clearly hear the announcer's deep voice over the hum of the motor.

"Stay with me, folks, right here on SASK radio. After the weather, to kick off the love-filled month of February, I'll select the winner of today's prize—a pair of tickets to tonight's Sweetheart Tour, another adventure hosted by Merilee Tours...a fun way to get away any day."

The announcer delivered Merilee's slogan with dramatic emphasis. An escape from exhausting days and a little excitement in her mundane life sounded appealing...if only she had the oomph. She sighed. Where did lively Jill go? A quick glance in the rearview mirror revealed faded, brown eyes and blotchy, pink circles from the cold on the cheekbones of her round face. She really needed to shake off the doldrums.

Shivering, she breathed bursts of cold air and cleared her head of the noise and motion of her grade five class. Most of her students were cute, but they sapped her energy, and she anticipated a quiet evening of TV sitcoms. She'd plunk on the couch and munch a bowl of popcorn beside her golden retriever, Georgia.

Memories squeezed her throat. When she started her teaching career twenty-five years ago, she never ran out of steam, even after a full day in the classroom. Back then, she overflowed with energy and embraced her fulfilling career and newlywed life. But three years ago, she wilted like a thirsty plant. Her divorce from Wes—a mutual but painful decision—knocked her right off balance.

Scanning for stray kids, she shifted into Reverse. The low, brick school lay ahead across the schoolyard, bordered by snowbanks and zigzags of footprints. Jill braked to let a car pass and then backed out of her parking spot into a white cloud. After a quick stop at Omar's Foods to pick up dog food for Georgia, she'd head for home, ready to settle in for the evening.

"Heavy snowfall and high winds could hit late this evening over much of the southern part of the province." The announcer enunciated each word. "Take care on the roads."

Bumping over ruts on the short drive to Main Street, Jill frowned at the weather forecast. No worries. Even equipped with snow tires, she wouldn't venture anywhere tonight, and she'd wake early in case she had to shovel a path from her doorway to the sidewalk and driveway.

"Now it's time for today's prize giveaway. Ready, Shauna?"

The announcer grabbed her attention. Shauna was her daughter's name, but out of all the listeners in this pocket of Saskatchewan, the caller couldn't be *her* Shauna.

"I guess so." Shauna laughed.

Jill would recognize her lively voice anywhere, and she smiled. Shauna might win.

"A leap year comes how often?" asked the announcer.

"Every four years."

"Congratulations, Shauna. Merilee will expect you on tonight's tour."

"Oh, wonderful. Thank you very much."

Shauna squealed her appreciation. She and her husband, Cody, were the spontaneous type, so they'd jump on the tour at a moment's notice. As soon as Jill walked Georgia, she'd call to say congratulations.

Her errand complete, Jill steered along quiet, snowy streets toward home. Inside the small foyer, enveloped by a current of warm air, she dove to greet her beloved dog.

Georgia wriggled in a circle and batted Jill's leg with her thick tail. The motion sent tufts of reddish-gold fur in all directions.

The scent of vanilla wafted from a trio of candles on a narrow table in the front hallway. Her modest bungalow, decorated in muted, earth tones, was an inviting, comfortable place.

A ring from the phone in her purse stopped Jill, and she rooted around and grabbed it.

"Momsy!"

Shauna beat her to the call. "I heard you on the radio. You won a nice prize." Jill bent and petted

Georgia.

"Yes, but would you believe Cody and I already bought tickets for tonight's tour? I called three friends, and no one is free to use them tonight. I can't waste my prize, so come with us."

"No, thank you, honey. I appreciate the offer, but I—" Jill rubbed Georgia's neck. A cozy evening with her dog suited her just fine.

"C'mon, Momsy. It'll be fun."

When had she last dropped everything for a little spur-of-the-moment fun? Even though she had drifted apart from Wes to a state beyond repair, after the divorce, she shrank into a safe cocoon at home. Still, the promise of a gourmet dinner and decadent chocolate made her mouth water. "But it's a romantic thing. I'll feel like a third wheel with you and Cody. You kids don't want me to crash your date night."

"If we minded, I wouldn't have invited you. We'll pick you up at five-forty-five p.m. to catch the bus at the Rec Centre."

"But the weather forecast—" Jill stiffened. Stubborn Shauna should listen and respect her wishes.

"See you then." Shauna clicked off the call.

Jill's peaceful evening evaporated into a cloud of uncertainty. Who in their right mind joined a romantic tour as a single? Hanging out with a busload of couples in love would only rub in what she lacked, even though by choice. Taking a deep breath, Jill hung her gray, down jacket, tugged off her black, woolen hat, and tossed it to Georgia to carry in her gentle mouth.

Staring at herself in the hallway mirror, she forced a smile. Sure her face was rounder than it used to be, but with the corners of her mouth upturned, she still looked youthful enough. She ran her hands over her waist and hips and winced at the soft bulges loitering there like unwanted visitors who stayed far too long. The extra flesh must go. All it did was drag her down.

She flicked her hair into place and spotted a few strands of gray threaded into the light-brown waves that grazed her shoulders. Before Shauna nagged, she should book a trim and highlights, but she would worry about an appointment later. Right now, even before she walked Georgia, she'd call Audrey. Her older sister always told her to get out more, so she'd be happy to hear Jill's evening plans. Besides, Audrey was best friends with Merilee, the tour host, so she'd know all the event details.

Jill flopped on the living room floor next to Georgia and tapped in the number of Goldview Gifts, the tasteful store Audrey owned on Main Street. Audrey possessed everything Jill didn't—oodles of energy, a trim figure, and a nice husband. Her quiet confidence and serene temperament were a steady influence on friends and family.

"Hi, Jill."

Obviously, before she answered, Audrey glanced at Call Display. "Can you talk?"

"Sure. I don't have any customers at the moment."

"You'll never guess what happened." Hand trembling, Jill stroked Georgia's fluffy side. Why was she so nervous?

"I give up." Audrey chuckled. "Tell me."

"Shauna won tickets to Merilee's Sweetheart Tour this evening, and she insisted I join her and Cody." Jill pictured herself riding alone next to an empty seat and winced. "She didn't give me a chance to refuse, but now what? I'll be the awkward extra on a busload of couples. Help!"

"Hey, you'll be fine. I booked tickets for Kirk and me on tonight's tour, so I'll keep you company. Don't worry. We'll have fun."

"Oh, thank goodness, Audrey." For an instant, Jill brightened. "But I don't know…" Without a partner, she would still feel awkward. She swallowed like a teenager who waited for someone to ask her to dance.

"Did Shauna offer you the second ticket so you could invite a date?"

"A date? You're joking, right?" Audrey was supposed to make her feel better, not worse. A weak attempt at a chuckle caught in Jill's throat. After the way she suffered through Wes's indifference, the last thing she needed was another man.

"I mean a friend. Maybe another teacher?"

Jill sighed and rubbed Georgia's belly. "She didn't offer, and I didn't ask. I doubt anybody but single me would be available on such short notice." In the background, the bell on the store door tinkled. "I better let you get back to work."

"See you soon, little sis. You never know what might happen on a bus. Merilee and Ross fell in love on the Christmas Cookie Tour." Audrey laughed.

Jill ignored her teasing comment, but an odd tickle rippled up her spine. "Bye for now." She hit End, tipped flat on her back, gripped handfuls of hair on both sides of her head, and stared at the white ceiling. Who could she possibly meet but a busload of couples who all felt sorry for the lone single woman on board?

Chapter 2

What Jack told his brother: "I'm single by choice. Unfortunately, it's not my choice."

****

With five minutes to spare, Jack Ryan wheeled into the parking lot of the Goldview Recreation Centre. When Cody called to insist he use a spare ticket on the Sweetheart Tour, he didn't ask many questions before he jumped in his car for the forty-five minute drive from his home in Regina. He didn't get booked to substitute teach today, so he hit the gym and finished his workout early. With nothing better to do, why refuse a nice dinner, with or without a sweetheart? A rare night out would feel good. He'd dated off and on since his divorce ten years ago, but he never quite clicked with the right woman.

Jack jumped out of his car and loped across the parking lot toward the bus. A cluster of people huddled near the door, and the smell of exhaust hung in the cold air. If a guy wasn't careful, February weather in the prairies could freeze off certain body parts. He chuckled inside. Approaching the group, he caught the buzz of conversation and bursts of laughter. Should be a fun evening.

"Hey, Dad." Cody raised an arm and motioned.

Jack hurried to join Cody, Shauna, and another woman. Shauna's mother? They'd met at numerous family events, but she always stuck close to her daughter. She was no conversationalist. "Hi, kids. Jill, how are you?" He didn't expect to see her here. She must have nabbed the other half of the pair of free tickets.

"Hi, Jack." Hands in pockets, she shifted.

He raised his eyebrows and chuckled. "Don't use *that* greeting on an airplane."

She half smiled and made a sound in her throat.

If anything, it was a sympathy laugh. His neck prickled under the collar of his jacket. Sure, it was a lame joke, but women who stared and blinked more than they talked made him nervous.

"Let's climb aboard, and we can chat more." Shauna led the way.

"Hello. I'm Merilee. Thank you for coming." A woman dressed all in pink and red smiled and flung an arm toward the steps and the bus driver. "On the way by, say hi to the driver, better known as my special friend, Ross."

She looked like a human valentine and bubbled like a beer. Now *she* was the kind of woman who would liven up a party. Her blondish hair bounced around her shoulders, and her eyes shone green as a golf fairway. Too bad she was taken. The way she called Ross *special* left no doubt.

"Welcome, folks." Ross smiled and nodded.

Lucky him to attract a woman like Merilee. Wearing a thick, red sweater, the guy was pleasant and not bad looking, but still…what did Ross have that Jack didn't? Envy kicked up dirt in his chest. He never quite measured up the way he wished.

The air on the bus smelled damp from passengers'

boots and rubber flooring. A few women wore too much perfume, and the scent of flowers wafted in waves. Jostling down the aisle, he followed Cody, Shauna, and Jill past seats filled with couples of all ages. No single women on this trip, unless he counted Jill. But the chance of dating her was as unlikely as a hole in one and about as appealing as a day in a school library. Darn.

"Hi, Auntie Audrey and Uncle Kirk." Shauna stopped and almost caused a pileup in the aisle. "I didn't expect to see you. How fun!"

Cody nudged her on. "We're blocking traffic. Maybe we can all sit together at dinner."

"Hi, you two." Jill shuffled by Audrey and her husband, Kirk. "See you at the restaurant."

"Oh, Jack. Hello." Audrey smiled and tapped Kirk's knee. "Remember Cody's dad? We met at Cody and Shauna's wedding and then again at a Christmas open house at their place."

"Of course, I know Jack. Good to see you." Kirk stuck out a hand across Audrey.

"You, too." Jack nodded at Audrey and shook Kirk's hand. "I'll catch you later."

Cody grabbed seats with Shauna in a spare row near the back and pointed to the place opposite.

Jill threw a glance at her daughter and slid in first.

Even with Jill plastered as close to the window as humanly possible, Jack felt crowded. The problem wasn't the amount of space; it was the prickly vibes he couldn't miss. Stuck together this evening, he'd focus on the food and try not to offend Jill with more attempts at humor. The revving motor signalled they were about to depart, and he settled back in his seat. Following

Jill's example, he held straight as a tree trunk and tucked in his elbows and knees to avoid touching her arm or leg.

"Good evening, everyone, and welcome to my very first Sweetheart Tour." From the front of the bus, Merilee waved. "Many guests told me my Christmas Cookie Tour was a highlight of the festive season, and I can't wait to make Goldview's Valentine's Day celebrations just as exciting and special." Holding the mic with one hand, she swung her free hand up and over her heart. "If you are here with your sweetie—which I'm sure is the case—you are in the right, romantic place."

Jack darted his gaze toward Jill and sensed her stiffen. No need to wonder her opinion. She was not with her sweetheart, and she wasn't pleased to have him squashed into the seat beside her. Slightly offended—he wasn't so bad, was he?—he dragged back his attention to Merilee's rapid, gushy announcements. Her over-the-top enthusiasm was a lot more fun than Jill's cold shoulder.

"I can tell you from personal experience, our driver, Ross, is a real sweetie. If we can do anything to make your evening more pleasant, please let us know." She tossed a smile over her shoulder in his direction.

Steering toward the gravel road out of town, Ross raised a hand and swayed it in a single wave.

"We'll make two stops to celebrate Valentine's Day—one for a delicious, three-course dinner and another for the most decadent, chocolate dessert you've ever tasted." Smiling, Merilee paused and scanned the rows. "How does that plan sound?"

The group applauded, and a few cheers burst out.

Jack contained a shrill whistle. Jill wouldn't appreciate the sound this close to her left ear.

"Now, before we cuddle up with a selection of love songs, I have an important question."

The busload hushed.

Jill's slow, deep inhale and exhale sounded like she was in a yoga class where she meditated until her stress dissolved. Was his presence really so hard to take?

"What do you call a very small valentine?" Smiling, Merilee scanned the rows.

He waited for the punchline. A few chuckles bounced over the aisle.

"Do you give up?" Merilee laughed, lowered her mic, and then lifted it to her mouth. "A valen-tiny."

Laughter and a few groans travelled over the group.

Jill joined in.

Maybe now she'd relax so she didn't arrive home with a kink in her stiff neck. He'd do his part and behave as best he could.

"All right, everyone. Please, sit back, and enjoy the ride. We'll arrive at our dinner spot in approximately thirty minutes. I think you'll be very pleased with the setting. For the information of those who haven't visited Prairie Hollow, it is an award-winning restaurant located in a historic home in the countryside. And now, I'll leave you to enjoy the music and your valentine." Merilee flipped her pink skirt and blew a kiss.

Careful not to bump Jill, Jack shifted in his seat and unzipped his jacket. The drippy notes of a love song floated from speakers. Maybe he should have asked Cody more questions about what to expect because he sure didn't bank on a lovey-dovey event.

He'd like to meet the right woman, but he wouldn't find her here. He cleared his throat. "How's the outlaw?" Maybe a safe, open-ended question would break the ice.

Jill jumped and glanced sideways, then straight ahead.

She acted like he poked her in the ribs. Instantly, a memory jabbed him in the side. He was the kid everybody rejected. Back then, nobody noticed the person underneath the flab.

"You mean in-law?"

Shrugging, he smirked. Why quibble? "In-law. Outlaw. Whatever. You know what I mean. We're related somehow through the kids."

"Oh, now I understand." She glanced over and offered a small smile. "This outlaw is fine, thank you." She paused and stared out the window. "How are you?"

"Darn uncomfortable, to be honest." Chuckling, he shook his head and drummed fingers on a knee. "We have our kids to thank. Cody mentioned dinner out. He didn't say I'd land in the middle of a lovefest. Free dinner grabbed my interest. What about you?"

"I read the poster, so I realized Merilee hosted a tour for couples." She folded her hands in her lap. "But Shauna wouldn't take no for an answer, and Audrey insisted I'd have fun with her and Kirk. So, here I am." She took a shaky breath. "I feel like I'm on a blind date."

"Yeah. Me, too." He laughed a bit louder than he intended. "Come here often? Like the music?" Personally, he could do without the sappy violin sounds that vibrated into his ears.

"What astrological sign are you?" Jill stared ahead.

In the dim lighting, Jack caught her smirk.

Encouraged by her contribution to the joking, awkward questions a couple might ask on a first date, he forged ahead. "Hey, baby, going my way?" Checking her expression, he snapped shut his mouth. Judging by the flush on her round face, he should have quit while he was ahead. He assumed she didn't mind the banter, but he guessed wrong. He should have bitten his tongue before he called her baby. Now what?

Mellow, guitar music filled the gap of silence. He wracked his brain for something witty or interesting to say, but nothing jumped to mind. He glanced at his watch. Fifteen more minutes until they arrived at their destination. His stomach growled. If he wasn't so hungry, he'd dread the dinner even more.

"I remember you teach school. Shauna mentioned you're a sub now."

Atta girl, Jill. Her quiet voice broke the tension, and he breathed a little easier. "Yep. Just call me a sandwich." He laughed and waited for Jill's reaction. "You look like the type who enjoys a good submarine. What's your favorite kind?"

"Pardon me?" She pursed her lips and tilted her head. After a few seconds, she hugged her arms around her middle. "Oh, ha. I meant sub as in substitute teacher."

She wasn't very amused by his latest attempt at humor. A knot of uncertainty tightened in his chest. "You're right. I substitute teach now. At my last school, I rubbed the principal the wrong way, so we agreed I should leave. Subbing is okay. It gives me more time to work out." He flexed his arms. "I lift more weight than most guys my age." Did she even notice his physique? After years as a fat guy, he'd worked hard to change.

"What happened with the principal?" She crinkled her forehead.

"I challenged him to lose weight and get in shape. Told him if he doesn't change, he'll die young. He didn't appreciate my advice."

The bus shuddered and rattled.

"Oh, I see." Jill inched closer to the window.

"Maybe I'll land a contract at another school. I'm fit and like kids. Guaranteed, I'd add a lot to any school's Phys Ed program.

"I'm sure." Jill stared ahead.

"Are we there yet, Mom?" Enough talk about work. Jack did his best impression of a child anxious to arrive. The knot in his chest grew and took up more space. Why didn't his athleticism impress her more?

Jill opened her mouth and closed it.

The woman sent mixed messages. Couldn't she take a joke?

"Hello again, folks." Merilee lowered the volume and chimed in.

A break from yet another sugary song, her lilting voice grabbed his attention. She spread enthusiasm as sweet and thick as jam on toast. The contrast with Jill was night and day. Jill's quiet demeanor was more like vanilla pudding—pleasant but plain.

The bus slowed and jostled Jack in his seat, and he braced himself so he didn't bump Jill.

"Sorry to interrupt your cuddle time, but we're about to arrive at Prairie Hollow." Clasping the mic with both hands, Merilee singsonged her important announcement. "Your tables for two are ready and waiting."

The murmur of happy voices wound up, over, and

between cozy couples. Jack couldn't miss the wince that flitted across Jill's face, and he fiddled with his jacket zipper. He should have declined Cody's invitation. Hungry or not, he'd rather wait alone on the bus than suffer through a tense meal.

He and Jill were opposites, and conversation didn't flow. Already, he sensed she didn't appreciate his quips. She didn't notice or care he was stronger and fitter than most guys his age. He sported a full head of hair, too, with not much gray mixed into the sandy blond. Couldn't she see he was attractive enough and a decent guy?

He slid out of the seat and sniffed the scent of cold, outside air that rushed down the aisle. "After you." He backed up and swung forward an arm to invite Jill to go ahead. Waiting in line, he rotated his tight shoulders. How would he survive dinner at a table for two with a woman who, obviously, didn't enjoy his company?

Chapter 3

Advice from Merilee: "Gentlemen, never laugh at your wife's choices. You are one of them."

****

Jill followed the line of passengers off the bus, with Shauna and Cody ahead and Jack behind. Others probably noticed Cody's blue eyes and sandy hair mirrored his dad's, the same way Shauna's brown hair and caramel eyes resembled Jill.

"Enjoy your meal." Ross offered a hand to anyone who needed assistance.

Merilee and Ross were a lovely, welcoming couple. They weren't to blame for Jill's failure to decline Shauna's last-minute invitation. Under different circumstances, one of their tours might be a refreshing getaway, but this evening, she'd just make the best of a bad situation.

Outside in a brisk wind, Jill breathed cold air filled with the clean smell of winter. Open prairie surrounded the sprawling, two-story clapboard home, now known as Prairie Hollow. In the dusky light, gusts of wind whisked snow against the white siding and blurred the outline of green shutters.

"Brrr." Jill shivered and pressed her arms against her sides to stop a biting draft from sneaking inside her jacket. Like the ice crystals that brushed her face, a pinch of concern prickled the back of her neck. The weather was more blustery out in the middle of the countryside than back in Goldview, and the forecast predicted heavy snow.

Jill hustled toward Shauna, and her swirling apprehension stole her breath. She shouldn't have agreed to come. Now she was trapped on a tour for couples and paired with Jack Ryan on an unnerving, accidental date. Bad weather only added stress to an already awkward situation.

Inside the restaurant reception area, Jill savored warm air laced with fragrant spices. Glancing around, she admired the cozy, old-fashioned surroundings. The walls glowed a rich cream with trim as deep gold as a wheat field. Old-fashioned, brass light fixtures shone an amber glow over the space. Sepia-tone photos of prairie scenes added to a nostalgic, homey feel.

"Welcome to Prairie Hollow." A young woman smiled and scanned the group.

"Hello, everyone. I'm happy to see you." Another young woman bustled to her side.

They must be sisters. With blue eyes and blonde hair twisted into buns, they looked enough alike to be twins, and their vintage, brown-and-gold dresses perfectly matched the décor. Laughter and voices vibrated through the congested space.

Somehow, Jill lost sight of Shauna in the crowd, and she scanned until she spotted the back of her curly, brown hair. If she threaded closer to Shauna, she would suggest they sit together. Her daughter couldn't abandon her now.

Audrey chatted with Kirk and another couple on the far side of the room. She raised a hand and waved but made no move toward Jill.

Audrey was sensitive and thoughtful. Surely, she wouldn't forget about her single sister. For a moment, Jill shrank into a high school wallflower, instead of a mature teacher and capable mother. Her temperature rose along with her stress level. She needed to remove her jacket before she dissolved into a blob.

"Here." Jack held out a hand. "Let me. My coat check services are cheap. I just take large tips. Twenty bucks will do." He laughed and raised his eyebrows.

Had he read her mind? "Thanks, Jack." She allowed a little laugh, slipped off her jacket, and handed it over. She tugged down the hem of her black sweater and smoothed it over the hips of her flowing, black pants. At her neckline, she wore a sparkly, silver necklace, designed to draw attention upward, away from her bulging waistline, round hips, and thick thighs.

She ran a hand over her soft belly, as if she could smooth away the extra flesh. Not that his opinion mattered, but Jack—Mr. Fitness—must notice her shape. A wash of disgust spiralled from her burning chest to her hot cheeks. She was sick of camouflaging her out-of-shape body and tired of feeling exhausted. In the three years since her divorce, she had paid little attention to diet and exercise, and the pounds crept up. But now, she missed the old Jill. She would reform her bad habits and reclaim her energy and joie de vivre.

Dropping her hand from her stomach, she hesitated. She wanted to join Shauna and Audrey but stayed rooted on the spot. She couldn't be rude and scuttle away on Jack. Waiting, she inhaled a deep, calming breath. The savory scent of roast beef wafted from the kitchen and made her mouth water, but at the same time, she couldn't ignore the nervous flutter in her stomach. Her appetite might not be as good as usual.

"Jill, what a nice surprise!" Nola Bergen, the Goldview School principal, appeared out of the milling crowd. "I didn't expect to see you here this evening."

Nola's breezy approach served her well with teachers and kids. Her silvery bob swung whenever she nodded, and her soft-gray eyes invited people to relax. Her wide smile was contagious. "At the last minute, Shauna surprised me with a ticket." Jill smiled and glanced over her shoulder.

At that moment, Jack returned, rubbing together his hands. "Dinner smells good." He faced Nola. "Hi, I'm Jack Ryan, Jill's date for the evening." He winked and chuckled.

Nola widened her eyes and smiled. "You didn't tell me you have a new man in your life."

"Only because I don't." For an instant, Jill lowered her gaze, and she resisted the urge to cross her arms. An odd combination of indignation and amusement rose in her chest. "He only wishes." She laughed. Did her remark sound flirtatious? She didn't intend it that way. "Seriously, Jack is just a friend…a relative, in a way. He's Shauna's father-in-law."

"Lovely. Well, you two enjoy your dinner. I better scoot back to Doug."

"Thank you for checking my coat." Jill glanced up at Jack, and the intensity of his blue eyes splashed her like water. She lowered her gaze to his brown, winter boots and took a step backward. Forcing her gaze upward, she swept over his dressy jeans and navy-blue sweater. A light-blue shirt collar peeked out at the neckline. "I'd like to catch up with Shauna and Cody."

"Sure. Hey, I checked your jacket all right." Jack clapped together his hands and grinned. "No money in any of the pockets."

"Heh. Sorry to disappoint you." She flicked a small smile and motioned with her head. "Let's go." Why did Jack try so hard to prompt a laugh? He reminded her of the boys in her class who acted goofy to get attention. He'd probably follow like an eager puppy at her heels.

At a tap on her shoulder, Jill swivelled and faced Yvonne and Henry. The small, perky, gray-haired couple lived down the block. Jill often stopped by their yard to chat in the summertime but seldom encountered them during the winter freeze.

"Hello, stranger. How are you?" Yvonne hugged Jill and glanced at Jack.

Jill's face burned hot again. All she wanted to do was escape to the safety of Shauna's or Audrey's company for moral support, but she couldn't avoid her neighbors' curious scrutiny.

Yvonne tilted her head and scrunched her face.

Henry raised his eyebrows and stared.

"Nobody told me you had a handsome boyfriend." Yvonne bounced her gaze from Jack to Jill.

Not again. Now Yvonne mistook Jack as her escort. "Oh, don't start rumors, Yvonne." Jill patted the older woman's shoulder. Her red blouse had white trim like a valentine. "Jack is Cody's dad. We're just friends." She almost laughed at the term. Awkward acquaintances was a more apt description. "Enjoy your evening." Finally, Jill wound to Shauna and Cody.

Now Audrey had circled toward the doorway and chatted with Merilee.

Jill bent close to Shauna's ear and lowered her

voice. "Make sure to ask—" She didn't get a chance to finish her request, but Shauna must know she wanted to sit with her and Cody and not alone with Jack.

"Hellooo." Merilee stood on tiptoes.

The way she swayed and floated her arms over her head, she reminded Jill of a pink fairy.

"Could I have your attention, please?" Merilee clapped three times.

The group quieted and focused on Merilee.

"Our hosts, Elin and Lars, will seat you now for your three-course dinner." She pointed at a tall, fair, middle-aged couple with modest smiles.

Like the pleasant, young women—probably their daughters—they wore old-style outfits that matched the era of the building.

"You'll enjoy soup, salad, and a choice of two entrees." Merilee ticked off the details on her fingers. "Enjoy your meal…and the special time with your sweetie." She giggled and swung her arms toward Elin and Lars. "Over to you."

The group filed in pairs led by their hosts.

"Don't worry, Mom," whispered Shauna, "We'll ask for a table together."

Just then, Audrey popped next to Jill. "About a table together…"

"Yes?" Maybe Audrey and Kirk would join them at a table for six. The more people to share in the lively conversation, the better.

"I talked to Merilee and—" Audrey shrugged and brushed Jill's arm.

"My little Cupid ears burned. Someone mentioned my name." Merilee swept in next to Audrey. "Jill and Jack, I'm so sorry. Much as I'd like to accommodate your request for a table for four or six, I can't."

Jill swallowed, and dismay churned in her chest. Why not? All restaurants shifted tables, didn't they?

"Elin explained the space is a little tight for a group of our size. The way Lars strung white lights and spread rose petals, he can't rearrange the tables and still leave a clear path for the servers." Merilee smiled and clasped her hands. "Please, forgive me." She swept her gaze from Jill to Jack, tilted her head, and shrugged. "I do whatever I can to please my guests, and I really wish I could fix things. But..." She smiled and touched Jill's arm. "Maybe you'll discover you like it this way."

Jill glared at Shauna and Audrey. They got her into this mess, and now she had no way to gracefully exit. For the next two hours, she'd sit across from Jack, listen to his boasting, dodge his wisecracks, and wrack her brain for neutral topics to pass the time.

Shauna cupped Jill's elbow. "You and I could dine together and leave Cody with his dad," she murmured.

Jill shook her head. Shauna and Cody paid a lot for tour tickets and deserved a special dinner date. As a loyal mom, she would bury her own discomfort for her daughter's happiness. She was a mature woman who would make the best of a bad situation. Maybe she and Audrey would laugh about it later. But still, how would she blot out the persistent strum of love songs and cope with her accidental, dinner date?

Chapter 4

A Sweetheart Tour joke: Did you hear about the near-sighted porcupine?

He fell in love with a pincushion.

****

"No problem, Merilee. Jill secretly loves my company. Take our names—Jack and Jill. We belong together." Mild apprehension tumbled in Jack's stomach, but he wasn't nearly as horrified as the expression on Jill's face. Her eyes shone as wide as two, full moons.

"I see what you mean—a real-life nursery rhyme." Crinkling her eyes, Merilee tossed her hair and laughed. "Well, Jack and Jill, I'll check in again later, but be careful. Don't fall down, Jack." With a little wave and a huge smile, Merilee flitted away to chat with other guests.

Jack joined the laughter from Shauna, Cody, and Audrey. He could survive this ordeal. He'd dealt with far worse as a bullied, chubby kid and later, as an unsure, overweight adult.

"Jack has a wild imagination." Jill smirked and hugged her arms around her middle.

"Wild is okay. A lot of fun." Jack fisted his hands, bent his elbows, and alternated a quick, forward-and-backward motion like a locomotive. "After dinner, we'll fill you in on the highlights. Right, Jill?"

24

Sometimes, joking made a connection with people.

Jill rolled her eyes and swiped a hand in his direction.

The group laughed again.

She brushed him off like a pesky fly, and her rejection stung his chest. He'd flinched at the familiar sting too many times in his life. But he looked at the bright side and found her agitation a bit funny. Maybe over dinner he could make her laugh.

Jill was too shy and reserved for his taste. But she was a teacher and raised a nice daughter, so she had a good heart. Her face was pretty in a natural way, especially when she smiled—a rare event. He didn't mind ample curves, and if she toned her body, she'd be quite attractive. He snapped back to the conversation in the room. Why did his mind wander in such a strange direction? Like Jill said, maybe he did have an overactive imagination. Even if she was his type, a relationship with his son's mother-in-law would be plain weird.

"I wonder what's for dinner." Cody patted his stomach.

Cody voiced Jack's unspoken question, and Jill probably appreciated the switch of topics. Yanked out of his daydream, Jack smacked his lips. "Whatever's on the menu, I hope the portion sizes are decent. I'm starved. Sometimes these fancy places skimp on quantities." Along with the rest of the group, he shuffled forward in the lineup to be seated.

"Please, follow me." Elin smiled and, skirt swishing, guided them to a table. "Enjoy your evening."

Settled in a formal, straight-back chair upholstered in textured, gold fabric, Jack sniffed the rich aroma of roasting meat and fresh-baked bread. Scanning left and right, he nodded at Shauna and Cody, seated across a narrow aisle, and Audrey and Kirk on the other side. Jill would probably appreciate the chance for a little interaction with the others. He didn't mind either.

"What gorgeous decorations." Jill gasped and scanned the room. "Look at the sparkly lights, white netting, and red roses...even petals sprinkled on the tablecloth and the carpet. I feel like I'm seated within a valentine."

Except for the overpowering, sweet perfume of the red flower in the centre of their table, he probably wouldn't have noticed the rest of the artsy details. Or should he say romantic touches? "Impressive." Now that he absorbed his surroundings, he meant it. Tiny, white lights swooped along the walls and twisted around plants in pink pots. Roses on every table transformed the room into a garden of red, pink, and white.

"Hello again. Happy Valentine's Day a little early!" Smiling, one of the young women in an old-fashioned dress presented a bottle of champagne. "I'm Ingrid, your server." She popped the cork. "Can I pour you a glass of bubbly?"

Jill nodded. "Yes, please."

"You don't need to ask twice." Jack slid over a glass.

Ingrid filled both glasses. "How long have you been married to this lovely lady?" She giggled and slid her gaze from Jill to Jack."

Jill popped her eyes wide and shook her head. "Oh, we're definitely not married." She leaned back in her chair and hugged her arms over her waist.

"She's just my girlfriend." Jack winked and chuckled.

Jill jerked forward and, with a sharp inhale, dropped her jaw. "Don't believe a word he says."

A glimmer of amusement flitted across Jill's face. Her light-brown eyes glinted in the flickering light of the candle. Jack glanced up at Ingrid, smirked, and shrugged.

"I'm sorry. I shouldn't have assumed you're married. Please, enjoy your date." She set down the bottle. "I'll come back to take your order." Ingrid spun and glided away.

Now what? Champagne called for a toast. Out of the corner of his eye, he noticed Cody whisper something to Shauna and raise his glass. A faint clink travelled across the aisle over the buzz of conversation and laughter.

"Here's to…" Jack raised his glass and paused. To what? To Valentine's Day? Too much romance involved. To February? Didn't make sense. To winter? Not when most people liked to escape one of the coldest months. He churned his brain for something appropriate. He didn't want to add to Jill's discomfort. "To teachers." Should be safe and not too personal but something they shared in common. Gripping the stem, he swung forward and instead of a gentle tap, he caused a midair collision. Glass snapped, and champagne sprayed his hand.

"Oh, no." Jill jumped, and, still holding the stem of her shattered flute, she gasped and raised her napkin.

"Jill, I'm sorry. Are you okay?" Embarrassment flipped in his stomach. How could he be so clumsy?

She nodded.

"Momsy, what's going on over there?" Shauna spun to face Jill.

"Never mind, Shauna. I'm fine." Jill waved her off. She dabbed her hand and the tablecloth.

Her mouth shaped like an O, Audrey swivelled in her chair and stared.

"Hey, you rowdies, settle down." Kirk tossed over his napkin.

"Go easy on the poor woman," Cody joked, but he crinkled his forehead and shook his head.

"Good advice." Jack chuckled but stiffened. His neck heated like a sunburn. He was coordinated and confident on the golf course and in the school gym, but he sure bungled the start of dinner. He wanted to kick himself under the table.

"Please, don't worry. Accidents happen." Within seconds, Ingrid gathered the pieces, whisked on a fresh tablecloth, and filled new flutes.

"I see you're out of trouble." Cody paused his conversation with Shauna to shoot a comment at Jack. "Try to behave now, Dad." He laughed and shifted back toward his wife.

"This time, maybe we'll skip the contact." Taking extra care, Jack raised his glass. "Here's to a fresh start with no more unpleasant surprises."

"Good idea." Jill smiled and followed his lead.

A trace of amusement skipped across her face, and her eyes deepened a shade to the color of milk chocolate. He liked chocolate. Although he'd met Jill in the past, he'd never really studied her facial features. Now, he welcomed the sight. If he handled the conversation right, he could learn a lot more about this reserved woman over dinner. The next two hours could prove very interesting. Maybe his spill eased the tension, and he could drum up a decent conversation. But how did she feel about the view from her side of the table?

****

Jill sipped her champagne and perused the menu, printed on thick, pink paper framed with hearts. With the romantic décor, she couldn't forget for a moment love bloomed like flowers everywhere in this dining room, except at her table. Still, she faced two hours of one-on-one conversation with Jack, so she better, at least, try to enjoy the time.

Jack gulped a third of his drink and lowered his gaze to the menu.

From the slight vibration in his upper body, she guessed he bounced a knee, concealed by the thick, white tablecloth. He was a bit of a puzzle. He boasted and flaunted his fit body, and he desperately wanted to make people laugh. Sometimes his attempts at humor worked, but often they fell flat. Sudden empathy flooded her heart. When he broke the glass, his flushed neck and cheekbones betrayed his embarrassment. He wasn't as self-assured as he pretended.

Ingrid returned with a pen and pad to take their orders. "Ladies first. What would you like?"

Jill glanced up. "Seafood chowder, Caesar salad, and prime rib, please." She'd enjoy the dinner and worry about calories tomorrow.

"And you, sir?" Ingrid smiled at Jack.

"I like to keep healthy and avoid foods high in fat." Jack examined the menu. "So I'll choose the tomato bisque, mixed greens, and baked chicken." He glanced at Jill and handed his menu card to Ingrid.

Jill wanted to bolt from the table and savor her fat-laden meal in private. Just when she started to feel sorry for Jack, he showed no tact and threw out a veiled insult. He offended her on the bus with his remark about her fondness for sandwiches, but she excused it as an accidental blunder. Now, hearing his commentary on the reasons for his menu choices, she squirmed at her less-healthy selections.

Embarrassed by his implied criticism, Jill wanted to fan her face with her napkin, but instead, she sipped cool water and took a deep breath. The strains of a popular love song dipped and swirled over the room but didn't help her relax. She didn't belong in these surroundings with this man.

Shauna leaned over. "Dinner sounds delicious."

"It smells yummy, too." Jill nodded and inhaled the scents of garlic and basil floating from the kitchen. Maybe Shauna would be too busy enjoying her own food to notice what Jill ordered. Jill sucked in her stomach. Like Jack, Shauna might disapprove of her menu choices. Wearing dressy jeans and a red sweater, Shauna was trim and fit like former Jill. She suggested healthy activities and low-fat recipes all the time.

Shauna straightened and picked up her conversation with Cody.

How wonderful to be young, married, and in love. Those days were a distant memory. After the sad unravelling of her marriage, she frequently counselled Shauna to always make her relationship a priority and never grow apart from Cody.

Audrey glanced over, smiled, and then continued to chat with Kirk.

Suddenly, Jill's ribcage squeezed too small. She

envied her sister's life. Kirk was the kind of devoted husband any woman would be lucky to marry. Early on, Jill adored Wes, but she soon realized although he was a solid dad, he was a disinterested husband. The whole, painful experience left her burned out and disillusioned. Taking a chance on another man would likely only lead to more heartache. She'd probably never reclaim the joy of youth or the happiness Audrey enjoyed.

"Chowder for you, ma'am, and the bisque for you, sir." Smiling, Ingrid balanced a tray and served steaming bowls.

"Thank you." Jill nodded and swept her gaze from Ingrid to the soup.

"Please, let me know if you need anything at all." Ingrid spun and glided away toward the kitchen.

Jill sipped a spoonful of the rich, creamy liquid and savored the salty, seafood flavor. "Mmm. Delicious."

"Mine, too." Jack scooped several mouthfuls and glanced up.

Jill squeezed her free hand around the napkin on her lap. Somehow, she'd make small talk through three courses.

At a leisurely pace, Ingrid gathered their empty bowls and presented salads followed later by entrees.

"Besides teaching, what keeps you busy?" Jack set down his fork.

His simple question caught Jill with her mouth full, and she paused to swallow. "I exercise my dog, Georgia. She's a loyal companion."

"I like dogs but don't have one. What else?" He gulped his champagne.

"Hmmm. Nothing special. I bake cookies and pies. I read a lot and visit Shauna and Cody. Audrey and I get together a couple of times a week." She speared a piece of meat and swirled it in the sauce drizzled over her plate. The enticing aroma of red wine and thyme drifted upward. "A few years ago, I swam a lot and curled on a team but not lately. I sold my bike because I never rode it."

Why did she leave most of her hobbies in the past? Adjusting to single life, she found solace in food, and the less she exercised, the less it appealed. After a while, she settled into a comfortable but lonely, couch-potato existence.

The music playlist wandered into a mellow song, even more heart tugging than the last. She breathed but couldn't quite fill her lungs. Too much heaviness piled on her chest in a smothering heap. Jack's question shone a light on the way her lifestyle had evolved and the changes she needed to make. He must find her very boring.

"Now, your turn. What do you do besides teach and work out?" No doubt, he'd love to expound. She wrung her napkin in moist hands. Just a few more bites of earthy, roasted vegetables and juicy, rare beef would finish her dinner. Then they could board the bus and travel to the final stop on the tour.

"I cross-country ski, golf, and play tennis—whatever burns calories so the pounds don't pile on."

Jack puffed out his chest so far he might pop the buttons on the shirt underneath his sweater. He was proud of his results, which was fine but also wore her out. "I plan to get fit again." Irritation jumped from Jill's stomach to her temples. He didn't need to feel superior. She gripped the arms of her chair and shifted her hips and thighs.

"You won't regret your decision." Jack swallowed the last bite of his chicken.

She nodded but still looked forward to a treat. Dessert awaited at another well-known restaurant. "I hope the stormy weather doesn't hit before we arrive back in Goldview."

"We'll be fine." Jack set aside his napkin. "People worry too much about the weather. A little, prairie storm won't stop Ross."

"If you say so, Jack." Jill didn't agree, but she wasn't about to argue." Instead, she pursed her lips and thought about school report cards instead of the piano sounds of yet another love song. Between the music and the conversations, the room jumped to life and throbbed with a warm atmosphere—a little too much for Jill's taste. Searching for a new topic, she spotted Merilee winding among tables.

"Hello, everyone." Merilee positioned herself near the dining room door and waved a hand overhead. "Did you enjoy your dinner?" At the group's enthusiastic applause, Merilee beamed, clapped together her hands, and rolled forward onto her toes.

Now, more envy stirred in Jill's very full belly. Would she ever feel so energetic and happy she'd perform her own version of Merilee's joyful, little bounce?

"My sweetie, Ross, is ready and waiting to drive us to our next stop…for delicious, decadent dessert." Merilee motioned to follow her outside.

"Thanks for being my dinner companion." Jack slid back his chair and gestured for Jill to lead the way.

"You're welcome. I enjoyed it." She'd leave Jack to interpret whether she meant she liked the food, the conversation, or the company. Certainly, the meal was first class, but the overall experience left her a little unsettled. She survived part one of the evening. Now, how would Jack complicate part two?

Chapter 5

A Sweetheart Tour joke: What did the chef give his wife on Valentine's Day?

A hug and a quiche.

****

Jill hunched her shoulders and hurried to the bus. The wind had picked up and whipped snow in sweeping gusts against the restaurant and over the field beyond. If Ross found the driving visibility poor, he might need to turn back toward Goldview. If the tour continued, she'd be forced into more time with Jack.

"Let's mix up the seating, Cody. I'll sit with Mom." To the strains of a rom-com movie soundtrack, Shauna slid into the seat beside Jill. Lowering her voice, she leaned in. "I'll give you a break."

"Thank you." Jill wanted to hug her on the spot. She could use a chance to relax for a few minutes. Taking a deep breath, she breathed the damp-smelling air. She peeked outside through a frosty window. Snow blurred her view, and faint concern tapped in her temples. Nobody wanted to travel through a Saskatchewan storm.

With everyone on board, Merilee jiggled, flipped her pink skirt, and picked up the mic. "Welcome back, everyone. Ross will keep a close eye on the weather so we stay safe." The bus rolled forward. "We'll stick with our plan to continue fifteen minutes down the road to our dessert stop. It's a bakery called Cake & Bake, and you'll love it. We visited there on my Christmas Cookie Tour, and all my guests were very impressed with the delicious baking."

"Jack likes you," Shauna whispered.

"Maybe as an outlaw. He uses that label to describe the way we're almost related but aren't exactly in-laws." In the darkness, Jill's face burned. He liked to tease, but did he really think she was somebody special?

"No, I mean he *likes* you. Even Cody notices how he tries to impress you.

"Like when he broke his glass and spilled champagne all over our table?" Jill laughed and raised her eyebrows. "Wasn't dinner fabulous?" She switched topics and diverted Shauna's attention.

"It was delicious." Shauna rubbed a hand over her stomach. "I'm so full I don't think I'll have room for dessert."

"When you see it, you might change your mind." Jill glanced out the window at the worsening weather and shivered. "The way the bus is crawling I feel like we'll never arrive."

After a slow trip, Ross parked in front of a mint-green building in a row of quaint, pastel shops. Snow trimmed the roof and windowsills like icing on a cake.

"Go right in, folks. Hang your coats, and choose a table for two." Merilee waved everyone off the bus. "Watch your footing. Sometimes, ice hides under the snow."

Inside Cake & Bake, Jill paused and brushed snow off her jacket. Warm, sweet aromas hugged her and hinted of mouth-watering desserts. She tapped Shauna's shoulder. "Sit with Cody. I can handle Jack for another hour."

"Are you sure?" Shauna touched her forearm.

"Absolutely." Uncertainty fluttered in Jill's middle, but she didn't need to let Shauna know. A guitar version of yet another sweet love song floated in the background. She scanned the décor and admired the little, pink lights that outlined the room and the pretty bunches of pink and white roses adorning the tables. The air hung dense and moist with the enticing scents of chocolate, vanilla, and flowers—all her favorites.

Jack swayed his arm and signalled he already selected a spot.

The seats were nowhere close to Audrey and Kirk or Shauna and Cody, but to her complete surprise, Jill didn't mind too much. She wove between tables and plunked down across from Jack. Something about the casual atmosphere made her feel more at home, and she propped her elbows on the table and rested her chin on her hands. "I love chocolate, so please, don't mention healthy eating." She smiled to soften her instruction.

"Yes, ma'am." Jack chortled and saluted.

The wrinkles that radiated from his eyes deepened, and his eyes caught the light and twinkled. His amusement sent a ripple of satisfaction into her chest. Maybe he wasn't too hard to like, after all. Since they shared a family and a career in common, she better tolerate the guy, even if she'd didn't feel any romantic interest.

Pangs of loneliness and regret punched her in the stomach. Her days were full, but most evenings were empty. She missed vibrant Jill, but only she could change her situation. She would never count on a man—even one the opposite of Wes—to complete her life, so she long ago squashed the idea of a new partner.

Glancing around, Jill breathed the sweet air. After dessert, she could finish her evening and head home, where she belonged. Searching for another topic of conversation, she traced the path of a woman wearing a pink apron who breezed through the room with a large tray of desserts.

"Hello, I'm the owner and baker, Beth." Pausing at their table, she presented the selection with a flourish.

Beth's round face and thick waistline reminded Jill of her own shape. "I'd like the chocolate chiffon cake, please."

"I'll have the lemon cheesecake, please." Jack grinned at Beth. "She promised to share her dessert."

Jill glanced up and huffed in mock exasperation. He kept her on edge. "Only if you trade."

"Deal." Jack slapped a palm on the table.

His voice rose above the murmur of other conversations. He grabbed attention like a teacher in class, but why the need to be noticed? Did he seek approval because he felt uncomfortable in his own skin?

"Remember the rule." Beth grinned and directed her comment at Jack. "Happy spouse, happy house. I'll leave you two to sort out the details on how you'll share."

"Oh, we're not mar—" Jill sputtered an explanation, but she faced Beth's back. Their host already whirled to serve the next guests. Why did everyone think Jack was her husband? Couldn't they see in this case, opposites did not attract?

****

Jack leaned across the table and stole a bite of cake right off Jill's plate. The rich smell of chocolate wafted from his fork and mixed with the lemon scent from his cheesecake. The combination was well worth an extra trip to the gym to burn off the excess calories. He'd make the most of this last, tour stop.

Jill dropped her jaw and pointed her fork. "Hey."

"Hey, what? You agreed we could share." He grinned at her wide-eyed expression.

"Okay, but let's be civilized and cut pieces with a knife." She sliced off a corner and slid it onto his plate. Then she served herself an equal share of his dessert. "Now you can keep your fork to yourself." She tasted a bite of cheesecake. "Mmm. I don't know which I like better."

"Why choose?" He sampled another mouthful of sweet chocolate.

"You're right. Why play favorites?" Jill licked lemon topping from her lip.

"Obviously, Beth doesn't." He tilted his head in her direction.

"Pardon me?" Jill widened her eyes and stopped chewing.

The realization hit him like a snowball. His comment offended Jill. "Oh, never mind." He shoved a large forkful of cheesecake into his mouth. Beth was plenty pudgy, but he didn't need to call attention to her size.

Jill narrowed her eyes and concentrated on her dessert.

"Tell me about your—" Jack was about to ask about Jill's class.

"Hello, everyone." Merilee called, swayed, and

waved both hands. "I need to make an announcement."

Murmured conversation and the tinkle of cutlery faded to a hush. Only the guitar chords of a gushy ballad broke the silence. Without other sounds, the music played too loud and too mellow for his taste.

Scanning the group, Beth hurried behind the display case and lowered the volume.

Merilee's face flushed pink like her outfit and the decorations. Behind her smile, her jawline and cheeks stiffened. Jack sensed—as much as witnessed—the tension, and her usual sparkle faded just a touch.

"First, do you agree Beth's desserts rate right up with Saskatchewan's finest?"

The group clapped and smiled.

"Here's to the baker," somebody—possibly Kirk—shouted.

"I'm so glad you enjoyed sweets with your sweetheart." Merilee crossed her hands over her heart.

Jack glanced at Jill and caught a glimmer of an eye roll. Didn't she see the humor in the situation?

Jill tugged down the hem of her sweater over her hips and fixed her gaze on Merilee.

"Now, I have some good news and some iffy news. While we indulged in Beth's fabulous desserts, the wind and snow picked up. Ross just checked the weather reports, and I'm afraid we can't leave for home at the moment because the roads are treacherous, and visibility is nil. The forecast says the storm system should ease in the early hours of the morning."

A murmur rippled across the room.

"I'm so sorry for the inconvenience, but let's make it into a great adventure. Beth won't toss us out in the storm and will let us stay as long as we like. She'll even open the room used for private gatherings at the back of the building." Merilee scanned the group. "Please, make yourselves at home, and if you need anything, let Ross or me know. I'll update you as soon as I know more."

"What should we do for fun?" Jack rubbed together his hands. No one waited at home, and he'd have a good story to tell. He faced Jill and examined her face. She appeared a little droopy. "Past your bedtime?"

Jill checked her watch and stifled a yawn. "I might need coffee to keep me awake."

"Coffee? Nah. I know something that'll work way better." If he was stranded with a woman, he would make the most of the opportunity. "Do you like to line dance?"

Chapter 6

What a friend told Jill: "I want a man who looks at me the way I look at chocolate cake."

****

Jack insulted Beth's size. Jill was sure. She asked him to repeat his comment, but he backed down and wouldn't say it again. He realized he blundered and probably didn't want to offend her, but she knew full well what he meant. His flippant remark hurt as much as a poke in the side of her ample waistline. When this evening ended—whatever time they managed to escape the storm—at least, she didn't need to spend any more time in his company for months. The next extended-family gathering likely wouldn't take place until next Christmas.

"Excuse me, Jack." Jill grabbed the opportunity to escape his company. She scraped back her chair. "I need to make a phone call."

"Sure thing. I'll catch you later." Jack tossed his balled napkin onto the table and swung to his feet.

Jill slipped to the edge of the room and tapped in a neighbor's number. Rachel—an outspoken woman with frizzy, black hair and lively, teenage kids—kept a key to Jill's house and was always willing to dog sit.

"No problem," said Rachel. "I'll rescue Georgia right away. She can stay all night, so don't worry about a thing."

Jill sighed with a wash of relief. "You're a lifesaver. I owe you." Even though Georgia was a dog, she was family, and Jill would never abandon her overnight.

"That's what neighbors are for. Have fun."

Jill clicked End and scanned the bakery. The room swirled with a blur of color and chorus of voices. Apparently, she would spend extra time in the company of all these people. The quiet, romantic atmosphere gave way to concern about the weather and questions about when the tour might return home. With no more focus on couples, Jill took a deep breath and dropped her shoulders. Tension flowed away, and she relaxed more than she had all evening. In a casual group and not as a stiff pair, she belonged.

Jack wandered across the room to chat with Cody.

Jill narrowed her eyes. How could Jack grin and greet people like a long-time resident, even though he'd never lived in Goldview? Free to socialize with Shauna, Audrey, and others, she meandered around the edge of the room and joined a circle of women. "Does anybody have a deck of cards?" She laughed and tugged down the hem of her sweater to make sure she appeared as lean as possible, which was difficult, considering how much she just ate. The buzz in the room chased away her momentary sleepiness.

"Seriously, we'll need to do something to amuse ourselves." Audrey flipped over her hands so her palms faced up. "We might spend hours waiting for the storm to pass."

Audrey's brown eyes—a shade darker than Jill's—behind tortoiseshell glasses sent an aura of calm. Always quiet and steady, she would be a good influence on anybody too uptight about the situation. Her presence always soothed Jill. Without betraying any confidences, Audrey sometimes relayed humorous examples of how she saved Merilee from spinning into a frenzy. For such good friends, they were definitely opposites.

"I'm so tired I could curl up in a corner and nap." Shauna covered a yawn. "I had a busy work day, and I'll start again at eight in the morning, assuming we make it home by then."

Jill rubbed a hand up and down her daughter's back and examined her profile. The corners of her eyes drooped, and her round face was a little paler than usual. Come to think of it, Shauna acted more tired lately. Usually she thrived on activity but, recently, not so much. She better not turn into a younger version of Jill. Setting a good example for Shauna meant everything, so now, Jill counted another good reason to return to her fit, lively self.

"Let's sit over there." Jill pointed to a table in a corner. "Come and join Shauna and me." She glanced from Audrey to Nola and breathed the faint aroma of fresh, brewed coffee. Beth must want to keep her guests awake and happy. The playlist of love songs faded to the background until it was barely audible over the hum in the room.

"I'm so sorry about the weather." Merilee breezed into their circle and threw up her hands. "My sweetie, Ross, didn't want to take chances with your safety, which is one of the reasons I love him."

Merilee spun a whirlwind of words until she paused for a deep breath.

"I hope you'll still have fond memories of this

evening. Enjoy a beverage. Treat yourself to another dessert. Just make sure you have fun." She clapped together her hands. "Audrey, keep watch and make sure these ladies behave." She laughed and scanned their expressions. "Anyway, how do you feel?"

"Just fine, under the circumstances." Audrey spoke for the group. "Had I known what to expect, I might have packed my pj's and a good book, but don't worry about us."

"Please, help yourselves to coffee or tea at the counter." With a flip of her pink skirt, she bounced over to another group.

For a while, Jill listened to the others exchange Goldview town news, and then she stifled another yawn. She was too tired to contribute much to the conversation, but she might as well do something to keep herself awake. Shauna, on the other hand, looked too wiped out to fight sleep. "Let's drag a couple of chairs against that wall, and you can put up your feet and take a nap."

Her daughter didn't resist, so Jill helped her set up a makeshift lounge and threw a coat over her as a blanket. Peering out a window, she monitored the weather. Gobs of fresh snow smacked against the glass, and she squinted into a sheet of white. She spotted no sign the storm would taper anytime soon. Shivering, she sighed and followed the twangs of guitar music blaring from the back room.

Taking a tentative step into the doorway, she widened her eyes at the scene. The bakery's cute, pastel surroundings transformed into a rustic bar with a wooden floor, dim lighting, and weathered panelling on the walls. Brown tables for four rimmed the room, leaving a wide, open space in the center. A small group followed Jack's lead and line danced to a popular song.

Apparently, the quiet, romantic evening was replaced by pure, country fun.

"Jill, come and join us." Jack waved and pointed at the dance floor.

"No, thank you." Jill spun to return to the sedate, bakery atmosphere, but at a tap on her shoulder, she braked.

"C'mon. We'll have fun and shake off all those calories we consumed. You have nowhere to go and nothing better to do." Jack grinned and swung an arm toward the centre of the room.

She avoided his vivid, blue eyes. They drilled too deep for comfort, and at his reference to calories, her face heated. Did he intend to suggest she overate, or did his comment just reflect his own obsession with healthy eating? Either way, she wasn't impressed. About to escape, she bumped into a beaming Omar and his wife, Fatima, from the grocery store. They must have left their newborn baby with a sitter.

"Stay and dance." Fatima motioned with her fingers.

The couple's matching, dark eyes and wide, white smiles gleamed with such delight Jill hated to refuse. If a woman who gave birth barely six weeks ago—very nearly on Merilee's Christmas Cookie Tour—could strut her stuff, so could Jill.

"I'll be right back. I promise." Slight apprehension and mild excitement fizzed in her limbs. She hadn't set foot on a dance floor since her niece's wedding five years ago. She loved to dance, but it fell to the wayside without a partner—not that Wes was ever eager.

"If you don't show up, I'll send out a search party." Jack shuffled backward.

Jill bolted from Jack's scrutiny to round up moral support. Scanning the bakery, she spotted Merilee, head tipped back, probably laughing at something Ross said. Crinkly lines radiated from the corners of his eyes, and he stood tall and muscular with graying, brown hair. Their sweet attraction glowed like the moon. Love could spark at any age. If Merilee could meet the right man, maybe Jill could, too…someday. Pangs of envy and longing squeezed her heart. But wait. Why even daydream such a farfetched idea? She couldn't hold together her marriage with Wes, and she wouldn't risk similar pain with another man.

"Excuse me." Jill approached Merilee and Ross. She hated to interrupt their private moment, but she counted on Merilee for support. "Some of the group are dancing in the party room. Do you want to invite the rest to join the fun?"

"What a perfect idea!" Merilee threw up her hands. She rolled forward onto her toes and barely reached the height of Ross's chin. "Why didn't I think of it? Oh, I know. This handsome guy distracted me." She smiled upward and brushed a hand on his forearm. "Thanks for the tip, Jill. I'll announce it, and then we'll join, too. Right, sweetie?"

"Whatever you say, Mer." Ross shrugged and smiled.

For a moment, Jill faded into the background. She was a fly that flitted around a blooming love story. Audrey predicted Merilee and Ross would marry this summer. At the touching sight, she swallowed against an ache crowding her throat. "Thanks for your help. I'll see you in there." She better hurry back before Jack charged out to find her. On the way by Audrey and Nola, Jill touched their elbows. "Come with me, *please.*"

"Hello again." In the center of the bakery, Merilee gave three sharp claps. Noticing Shauna asleep, she hunched her shoulders and clasped her hands. "Oops." She lowered her voice to a stage whisper. "Everybody's invited to show us your fancy footwork in the party room."

Surprising anticipation danced in Jill's stomach. She tugged down the band of her sweater and led the way.

"Thatagirl." Jack flicked his eyebrows, fanned a toe, and glided into a step kick. Another popular country song strummed accompaniment. "I'll teach you a few moves, honey."

Jill flushed from her eyebrows to her toes. "I bet." She hustled to a row next to Fatima. The nerve of the guy. She wasn't his honey, and he had no business using the pet name. But she wouldn't let him bother her. She'd dust off her dancing shoes and show him she was no slouch. Already she could see by his sloppy steps, she could perform the hustle a lot better.

Step, kick, and grapevine. Jill caught the rhythm, floated with the rest of the line, and hopped in a quarter turn, right on the beat. Memories of younger days and spontaneous times rushed back as fast as a heel-toe step, and she laughed out loud. Pleasant warmth filled her chest, and she boogied until the last strum reverberated into the rafters, and she puffed for air. She hadn't shared this much fun in a long time.

The drumbeats and guitars faded, and Jack paused

and scanned the group.

Around Jill, nearly the whole busload of passengers stretched in rows across the floor. Catching her breath, she planted hands on hips, swivelled, and grinned at Audrey.

Audrey nodded and flashed a thumbs-up.

Nola shuffled over. "Nice style," she whispered. "I see you have talents besides teaching grade five." She laughed and sidestepped back to her spot next to Doug.

Facing the front, Jill swept her gaze over Jack. If he wasn't a little on the brash side, his looks would appeal. He was youthful for a guy of his age, and the gray streaked through his sandy hair hardly showed. She couldn't deny he appeared as fit as he claimed. With all the action to warm the room, he had peeled off his sweater, rolled up his shirt sleeves, and loosened the collar. His wide grin shouted joy, probably because his dance moves made him the center of attention. Jill squelched a smile. He must think he starred as the DJ and dance instructor, making everyone wait for his next choice of song.

In the silence, a faint whistle of wind seeped through the walls.

"Time for a polka. Grab your favorite partner." Jack headed straight for Jill.

A nervous quiver polkaed right to Jill's knees. She couldn't continue, could she? Line dancing in a group was nothing compared to close dancing as a couple. In Jack's arms, she'd whirl around the floor, jostle against his chest, and feel his hand on the small of her back. The whole idea unsettled her more than the blizzard outside. "No, thank you. I should check on Shauna. She's napping up front in the bakery."

"Don't worry. Cody will keep an eye on her. That's what good husbands do."

"But…" She hadn't danced a polka since before her divorce. She breathed the warm air, circulating faint scents of cinnamon and vanilla from the bakery. Remembering the giddy exhilaration of keeping pace with accordion sounds, she wavered.

Just as the playlist broke into one of the most famous polka songs, Jack clasped her hand and swung onto the dance floor.

The organ-like sound overtook her reticence, and she followed his lead. Hopping and spinning, she matched her rhythm to the music and synched with his bounces and swoops. His hand was so hot on her back it nearly sizzled. She floated in dizzying circles faster and faster, until she laughed and begged Jack to slow. She hadn't whirled this light and carefree in years. Finally, the music hit its final note. Puffing, she glanced at Jack, and her breath caught in her throat.

He stared deep into her eyes, blinked, and touched the tip of her nose with a gentle finger. "Well done."

Elation and confusion waltzed in her stomach, and her pulse raced. "I had fun. Thanks for the invitation." Shaken, she broke away and collapsed into a chair against a wall. For most of the evening, she had merely endured Jack's company. Now, why did she struggle to remove herself from his arms?

Chapter 7

SASK radio announcer on love: "Love is blind. Marriage is an eye-opener."
****

At eight the next morning, ready to impress, Jack strode into the waiting area outside Principal Nola Bergen's office at Goldview School. The bright, wide surroundings smelled like toast and coffee. The office staff must eat breakfast at their desks. Even though he ate already, his stomach rumbled.

"Good morning, Jack." Smiling, Nola shook hands and gestured to a chair in her office. "You appear wide awake for a guy who stayed up almost all night."

She looked alert, too, and professional in navy pants and purplish shirt. Good thing he wore khakis and a sweater and not gym clothes. "I feel okay. I only sleep if I don't have anything better to do." Chuckling, he sat opposite her. "Thanks for calling, Nola. I appreciate the opportunity." He glanced around her office. Framed artwork by students decorated the walls, and a bookshelf filled with colorful books stretched behind her desk. Through a large window to one side, the sunrise lightened the dark, morning sky.

"Thank *you* for agreeing to teach on short notice. With our late arrival home, I assumed you stayed in town overnight at Cody and Shauna's place." Nola smiled. "Welcome to our school, by the way."

How would Jill react when she found him here? Uncertainty rolled like a fitness ball onto his chest. He didn't mention to Jill he spoke to Nola about opportunities and left his contact information. He doubted Jill would have encouraged the idea. But he needed more work hours to fill his time and his bank account, and today's last-minute teaching assignment might give him the edge for an ongoing gig.

At three a.m., the group had cheered at Merilee's announcement the storm had eased enough to head for home. By then, even Jack admitted he was tired. After dancing until he wore out Jill and the rest of the group, he nursed a cup of decaf coffee at a table in the bakery. Finally, he hustled behind Jill, Shauna, and Cody back to the bus. The cold air bit his nose and cheeks, but at least, the wind didn't whip snow at his face. The street was deserted and quiet, and the passengers were too sleepy to talk or laugh much.

When Jill dozed on the bus, she tipped her head onto his shoulder.

The faint scent of her hair—like a flower garden, only better—quickened his breath like a jog around a gym.

As the bus slowed, she jerked upright and wiped the fingers of one hand along either side of her mouth.

"Don't worry. You hardly drooled on my shoulder at all." Jack kept a straight face, but a ping of attraction drove him backward in his seat.

Jill widened her eyes and slid her fingers over her mouth. "I didn't...did I?" She breathed in and out in a whoosh. "Please, tell me no."

Chuckling, he grabbed a tissue from a pocket and dabbed his shoulder. "Don't worry. My jacket is waterproof."

"Jack, stop." She laughed and leaned away toward the window so no part of her touched him.

The sound of her soft, hesitant amusement stirred an unfamiliar warmth in his chest. When the evening started, he considered her an unremarkable member of Cody's extended family. But now, attraction grabbed his chest. When he cracked an offbeat remark, he heated at the way she dropped open her mouth and widened her eyes. Her reaction made teasing even more fun. She wasn't the usual type who made his pulse race. But a few extra pounds couldn't hide her obvious intelligence, gentle personality, and feminine curves. On the dance floor, she had surprised him—in a very good way—and now, he daydreamed of more.

Jack yanked his focus back to Nola's instructions. The buzz of substitute teaching at an unfamiliar school and pleasing an unknown principal would chase away any sluggishness from his late night. Today's priority was to impress Nola so she would invite him back for a repeat performance.

While Nola outlined the job requirements, she nodded and smiled.

Her soft-gray eyes shone clear and bright. Her gray hair swung straight and smooth as a whiteboard, and she radiated energy and confidence.

"The position is eighty percent of fulltime. Today you'll teach four gym classes. Our regular teacher will soon take maternity leave, so if all goes well, I might offer you the chance to fill in for the next year."

Excitement surged in his chest. A whole year of teaching? Twelve months salary would boost his savings for a more comfortable retirement. He might have been a little optimistic about how far a teacher's pension stretched. With any luck, Nola and other teachers would view him as self-assured and capable. They'd never guess he was less confident on the inside.

A vague unease dashed through his stomach and dissolved. No way would he allow past hurts to drag down his confidence. He'd focus on the positives and anticipate good things to come. Near the top of the plus side of a continuing contract, he'd interact with Jill daily. Perfect, but what would she think?

"This list shows the day's timetable, grade level, and student names." Nola handed him several sheets of paper. "Just wait in the gym, and students will file in for their classes at the right time. You shouldn't encounter any major behavioral issues, but you'll soon figure out which kids need extra supervision."

Her smile reassured him he'd have a positive day. Not that he expected problems, but he found kids sometimes challenged a substitute teacher. He took a deep breath.

"If you have any issues, talk to the classroom teacher or me. Jill or I can introduce you to the rest of the staff at recess. Do you have any questions or concerns?"

"All sounds good." He pulled back his shoulders, stood, and nodded at Nola. She could rely on him to take over like a pro. Even though he sometimes didn't click right away with school staff, he cared about kids, which was the most important thing.

"No? Then I'll lead you to the gym and show you the equipment room." She ushered him out of her office and down the hall.

The walls beamed a cheery yellow with clusters of

bright artwork outside classroom doors. Students wouldn't arrive for a few more minutes, so the hallway waited empty. It smelled like lemon cleaner with a whiff of books, markers, and sneakers mixed in, just like every school he visited. So far, he spotted no sign of Jill.

Approaching the door of the gym, he glanced over his shoulder and inhaled a sharp breath.

Jill exited the classroom doorway opposite. She blinked and steadied her coffee mug with both hands. Staring, she opened and closed her mouth.

"Good morning, Jill." He paused behind Nola.

Jill's eyes and hair shone the color of wet sand. Along with her monotone, beige sweater and tan pants, she would blend with a stretch of beach. The combination might appear bland on the surface, but his erratic pulse shouted otherwise. He'd never have guessed one, long evening could make such a difference in his feelings.

"Oh, good morning, Jill." Nola spun to face her, too. "You know the gym as well as I do. Why don't I leave you to show Jack around? I don't know about you, but after our late night, I could use a second cup of coffee." She slid sideways. "Good luck, have fun, and I'll check in with you later." Nola smiled and raised a hand in a half wave.

"Surprise." Jack grinned at Jill. "You didn't expect to run into me this morning, did you?

"I didn't expect to see you until next Christmas at Cody and Shauna's holiday open house." She quirked an eyebrow and flickered a smile. "You returned ten months early."

"Don't sound so excited." He shifted and searched

her expression to decide if it was amused or agitated. Her scant smile gave no clues to her true feeling, but he would assume the best. Last evening, she had fun. Her face had glowed pink, and her eyes reflected amber in the yellow, party-room lighting.

"Come, and I'll show you where we store the equipment." She led him into the gym and pointed. "You'll find anything you need right in that little room."

Planting hands on hips, he sized up the space. Typical concrete-block walls and wood flooring painted with lines for basketball and other games surrounded him. The temperature cooled a few degrees from the hallway, and the smells of leather balls and rubber mats jetted him back to childhood, even though he had spent countless hours working out and teaching in similar surroundings. Young Jack didn't like the atmosphere at all. What were the chances a chubby kid would excel in—let alone like—gym class or intramural sports?

"You're just here for the day?" Jill scanned from his feet to his face.

She phrased her statement like a question. "If all goes well, maybe more. Nola mentioned a maternity leave needs to be filled."

"Oh." She raised her eyebrows. "I thought she already had someone in mind."

"Guess yours truly better fits the bill. If you get to see me every day, think of the fun you'll have." He grabbed a basketball off a shelf in the storage area and faked a pass.

Still holding her coffee mug, she tilted out of the way without spilling a drop.

"Nice move." He hugged the ball to his chest like a

round shield. "You're more athletic than…than I expected."

Jill widened her eyes and dropped her jaw. Then she strode to a bench along one wall and set down her mug.

He had stopped himself before he observed she was more athletic than she looked, but he still offended her. He didn't mean his comment to sound negative, only that her quick reaction was a pleasant surprise, just like her skills on the dance floor. "Sor—"

Grabbing another basketball, she dribbled toward a hoop at the end of the gym, sped into a layup, and sunk a perfect basket. Without a word, she fired the ball in his direction, retrieved her coffee, and paused in the gym doorway. "Have a nice day." She tossed the comment over her shoulder and disappeared.

Oh, great. She made her point he was a jerk. When would he learn to be more diplomatic and keep his big mouth shut?

Chapter 8

A valentine joke from the Goldview School announcements: What did one volcano say to the other volcano?

I lava you.

****

In the hallway, Jill paused to catch her breath. She escaped the gym before she showed Jack her impromptu basketball maneuver left her slightly winded. She'd cheered on Shauna at countless basketball games but hadn't played since her own high school days. Oddly, between dancing last evening and the toss of a ball today, she percolated with more energy than she had in a long time. She'd need to work hard, but she could reclaim her former, active lifestyle.

Jill settled into her classroom, scanned the kids' colorful self-portraits stuck to a side wall, and erased the blue writing on the whiteboard. Breathing air scented with markers, crayons, and sneakers, she straightened a row of books on a shelf near the back and took a few minutes before her students arrived to review her schedule for the day. At noon, the teachers would meet to finalize plans for the school winter carnival next week. At one fifteen p.m., her class would take their turn at gym class.

Clearly, she couldn't avoid Jack with his unwelcome observations and insensitive wisecracks. He irritated her…yet, somehow, she sensed he meant well. The uncertainty that flitted across his face reminded her of her student Oscar and the way he didn't quite fit in. Compassion and attraction whirled in her stomach. Jack's presence on the bus, at dinner, and on the dance floor stirred feelings that were only a distant memory.

The school bell jangled and interrupted her daydream. Laughter and footsteps reverberated along the hallway toward her classroom, and she inhaled a deep breath and switched back her focus to the day's agenda. Jack had no business stealing away her thoughts from her students. They were a lively bunch who demanded her full attention.

"Good morning, everyone. Hang your jackets, and get ready for a math review." She pointed to the hooks along the back of the room and hushed the groans. "What's seven times nine?" She scanned the room and landed her gaze on Oscar.

His brown hair straggled over his ears, and his T-shirt outlined the rolls down his stomach.

He was a smart kid but hung back as usual. Her heart twinged. A shy, overweight kid, he struggled to make friends, and more than once, when other kids teased him, she'd intervened.

"Uh…sixty-three," Oscar murmured his answer and stared at the table where he sat with two girls and another boy.

"You're exactly right." Jill smiled and flashed a thumbs-up. Oscar's round face flushed pink as an eraser.

He hunched his shoulders and fiddled with a pencil.

She worked hard to give him plenty of positive

feedback and help build his confidence.

Behind Oscar, pretty, black-haired Prisha wrinkled her nose.

"Prisha."

The girl jumped and widened her eyes.

Her innocent expression didn't fool Jill for a minute. "What is nine times eight?"

"Seventy-two." Prisha tossed her ponytail and stuck out her chin.

Jill glanced out the window. In the schoolyard, snow crystals glittered in the morning sun, and the only traces of last evening's storm showed in higher drifts and swirls on top of snowbanks. The hours until recess dragged yet sped. When she encountered Jack, she'd treat him with the same politeness she'd offer any colleague, but she wouldn't encourage his teasing, flirtatious behavior.

At the clanging of the bell, she sent her students outside and hustled toward the staff room. Fifteen minutes passed quickly. Teachers' and kids' voices skipped along the hallway, and the scent of strong coffee wandered overhead and enticed Jill to refill her mug. She paused in the lounge doorway and scanned the room for Jack.

Voices hummed through the staff room. A cluster of her peers chatted around the coffeemaker, and others sat around a long, cream-colored table. A few people relaxed on black couches at the far end of the room.

None of the groups included Jack. He'd hardly be too shy to join the group, but where was he? Setting down her mug on the counter, she spun and headed for the gym. Maybe he didn't know where everyone gathered at recess, and she hated anyone to feel left out.

Approaching the doorway, she heard the steady whack of running shoes on the hard floor before she spotted Jack as he jogged around the perimeter. He had swapped his streetwear for black sweatpants and white T-shirt, and workout clothes suited him. Surveying the scene, she hesitated to interrupt his intense focus.

He checked his fitness tracker and picked up his pace until he rounded the end and glanced up. As he approached, he slowed, grinned, and bounced on the spot. "I figured you'd miss me."

"Not exactly." She smiled to soften her remark, although he must know she teased. The way he dished out wisecracks, surely, he could take them in return. "But the teachers usually gather at recess, and you're welcome to join us."

"I'll see you at lunchtime. I like to exercise at breaks." He picked up his stride. "Feel free to join me. You might like it."

"Thanks, but no thanks." She contained a huff. Again, he pointed out her need for fitness. Did he realize how his comments stabbed her right in her rounded stomach? Her buoyant energy crumbled into a heap at her feet. Lumpy and out of shape, she didn't need Jack's reminders.

Returning to her classroom, she felt stubborn resolve rise in her chest. She'd change her ways, and she didn't need Jack's encouragement. But now, if he noticed her exercise, he'd probably take credit for the idea. Well, she wouldn't let his gloating stop her. Why did she interrupt her break to seek him out anyway? "Welcome back." She waved her students back into the classroom. They radiated the chill and scent of cold, outside air. "Oscar, would you like to choose our next book? I'll read aloud one chapter a day."

Oscar nodded and lumbered to the bookshelf.

At a whisper between two boys, she glared. Later she'd lead another discussion on how to be kind and respectful to one another. Kids could be sweet but also hurtful, especially to those who were different.

Immersed in her lessons, she didn't think again of Jack until the bell rang. She grabbed her bagged lunch and joined the rest of the teachers for the winter carnival meeting in the staff room. Surrounded by the aroma of pizza heated in the microwave, Jill unwrapped a chicken sandwich, carrot sticks, and an apple, all part of her recent, healthier food regime. She eyed another teacher's hot casserole and forced away her gaze from the delicious-looking dish. She wouldn't let it tempt her.

The staff filled chairs around the table and dragged in extras to expand the circle.

Glancing up, Jill scanned the room for Jack. Most likely, he'd show up soon, unless he spent his whole lunch break exercising in the gym. On especially cold days, she might walk inside during the noon hour. If Jack stayed at the school and hung out in the gym all the time, she'd either need to exercise elsewhere or accept his company. Suddenly, she heated in her sweater and hoped nobody noticed her flushed face.

"Let's get started. While I make notes, feel free to eat." Nola scanned the group.

With not a spare ounce on her tall frame, she stood crisp and professional as ever in navy pantsuit and burgundy shirt.

"We'll finalize the activities and then identify pairs of leaders to work with parent volunteers." Nola jotted a title on a flipchart.

Jill shouldn't worry about Jack, but she slid her gaze in a triangle from her food, to Nola, and to the doorway.

A few minutes into the meeting, Jack appeared, paused, and shifted.

Jill sensed his awkward hesitation, and an odd ache spread in her chest. His brash exterior faded and disappeared altogether. He must feel like an outsider with nowhere to sit and no one paying him any attention.

With her back to the door, Nola printed neat words in purple marker.

The group focused on their food or the flipchart.

The sharp scent of ink overtook the savory aroma of chicken and mustard from her sandwich. She picked up a carrot stick, crunched it in slow motion, and ran her gaze down from Jack's straw-colored hair and blue eyes to his hard body. Dressed in athletic wear, he looked younger than a semi-retired teacher.

She swallowed, and her heartbeat jumped. She couldn't deny he was attractive, especially for a guy of his age. Shoving aside his annoying cockiness, she couldn't let him just loiter in the doorway like a kid without a friend. In a motion so subtle likely nobody else noticed, she bent her right arm and pointed a finger toward a spare chair along a wall to the left.

Jack smiled and nodded. Clutching a brown paper bag, he skirted the room and slid into the chair.

"Oh, hi, Jack." Nola glanced up from her notes. "Everyone, this is Jack Ryan. He's filling in for Phys Ed class."

"Hello, all. I look forward to getting to know you."

He raised a hand in a half wave. "Sorry I'm late. I just helped a boy find his missing boots. I noticed a few others laughed at his predicament, so I roped them into the search. Funny, the loudest kid found it in about ten seconds."

Nola smiled and twisted the cap onto the marker. "I'm sure the student appreciated your help."

Jack's chuckle didn't sound amused. Jill picked up her sandwich and glanced over. His eyes crinkled in a fan on either side of his face. Were they lines of laughter or pain? Concern or compassion? Probably some of each. Jack had showed kindness to a kid who needed support, and she'd bet a chocolate cake the boy was Oscar. As the butt of his classmates' humor, Oscar often lost or misplaced belongings through no fault of his own.

Bullies had no place in Goldview School. She clenched her teeth and then forced them apart to chomp a bite of her sandwich. Crinkling her eyes, she sent an approving nod Jack's way. Obviously, he had the caring side a good teacher needed, so he possessed some redeeming qualities. She forced back her attention to Nola just in time to accept a role at the winter carnival.

"Jill, can I put you in charge of the snowball toss?" Without waiting for an answer, Nola printed her name in green.

"Sure." Jill preferred the hot chocolate station but didn't really have a choice, and considering her new focus on fitness, she didn't mind the chance to keep active.

"I'll help." Jack raised a hand before anyone else volunteered.

Jill waited for a wisecrack, but none spouted, and

she breathed a little easier. Teacher Jack refrained from his usual banter and showed more restraint than she thought possible. Maybe he wasn't so obnoxious, after all.

"Thank you, Jack." Nola smiled and added his name beside Jill's. "I might need to keep you around."

Sudden unease fluttered in her stomach, and she set down her sandwich. She had told Nola she and Jack weren't an item, and she'd stick to her word. Or would Jack change her mind?

Chapter 9

SASK radio announcer: "When you fall in love, that tingly feeling is your common sense leaving your body."

****

The moment she arrived home from school, Jill hung her jacket and dove to hug her golden retriever, Georgia, around her furry neck. Then she called Audrey at the gift store. Audrey would know how to handle the situation.

She flopped on the floor beside a square, cream ottoman and rubbed Georgia's fluffy belly. Some people didn't like the musky odor of a dog, but to Jill, it smelled like home. A plaque hung by the back entrance and made her smile every day with its playful wording—*Home is where the dog is*.

She didn't bother to ask if Audrey was free to talk. Her sister would let her know if she was too busy for a call. "You won't believe who subbed at school today," Jill practically shouted. She glanced at Georgia's golden coat and around the living room. The colors of the couch, chairs, and area rug all blended in muted shades of beiges and browns with nothing to jar her senses. Even Georgia matched the soothing palette.

"I give up."

Audrey's hushed tone suggested customers might browse within earshot.

"Jack Ryan."

"He followed you." Audrey gasped and, in the same moment, laughed.

Jill ignored her exaggerated, teasing reaction as though Jack was practically a stalker. "Apparently, he schmoozed Nola on the tour and convinced her to add him to the school's sub list. She hired him to cover gym classes today, and he sounds confident he'll nab a contract to cover a maternity leave for the next year." Anticipation and dread argued in her stomach. If she faced Jack every day, school life would be different, and right now, she couldn't decide if it would be worse or better.

"One day at a time, little sis."

Audrey's smooth tone should have calmed Jill but only stirred her agitation.

Georgia thumped her tail and licked Jill's hand.

Her loyal dog sensed something was wrong. "I don't like the way he flaunts his fit body and cracks comments about everything, even if the topic is none of his business. Now, he even invaded my territory at school." She sighed, and the scene in the staff room crept in and tapped her shoulder. Maybe her assessment wasn't totally fair but still… She stretched out her legs and examined her thighs. They weren't exactly tree trunks, but they sure weren't twigs.

"He's a lot of fun," whispered Audrey. "I talked Merilee into giving Ross a chance, and look how they clicked. Anybody can see they're in love. Now I want you to find the right guy, too, so why not give poor Jack a chance?"

Jill pictured her older sister, a steady fixture in her life. Nothing phased her. Audrey floated through her days and rose above petty concerns. Her tortoiseshell glasses and subdued, brownish wardrobe exuded a wise and comforting presence. Why didn't Jill inherit her share of calm? She might resemble Audrey on the outside, but she sure didn't share her qualities on the inside. "I'm an introvert. I like my own space. He fills it to overflowing." Even to her own ears, Jill sounded whiny.

"You were pretty happy on the dance floor."

Jill huffed. Sometimes Audrey focused too much on the bright side. "I had nothing better to do." But Audrey's observation was one hundred percent correct. Jill hadn't let loose in ages. So why did she want to avoid more time with Jack?

"Sorry, Jill. A customer needs my help." Audrey rushed her words.

Jill clicked off the phone, bent her legs, and hugged her knees, but in an awkward position, her waistline and hips bulged. "Ugh." She pronounced her disgust to Georgia, who loved her all the same. Rolling to her feet, Jill grabbed her jacket. "Let's go for a walk." Audrey offered no sympathy, but at least, Georgia listened without judgment. Well, Jill wouldn't sit and feel sorry for herself.

She hooked Georgia's leash, and at a firm rap on the front door, she straightened. Hardly anyone dropped by unannounced. She swung open the door and faced Jack. Pulse jumping, she widened her eyes and gripped the doorknob. Would the guy ever leave her alone? Now what did he want?

*****

Facing Shauna, Jack scraped forward his chair at Burger Town, the casual diner Cody owned. Last night's Sweetheart Tour marked a rare evening off for his son. Since Cody worked this evening, Jack invited Shauna to join him here for dinner. He'd pump her for insider info on her mom.

Jack glanced around. The diner was his kind of place. Oldies strummed from the sound system but not so loud he couldn't hear a conversation. The aroma of basic food like burgers and fries filled the air. Plenty of laughter topped off the relaxed atmosphere. He didn't mind the orange booths that framed the room, the clatter of dishes, and the jumble of voices. A swell of pride filled his chest. Cody worked hard to achieve his dream of owning a successful restaurant.

"Your mom's a great lady." With a loud spurt, Jack squeezed a pool of ketchup onto the edge of his plate.

Shauna poked her fork at a chicken Caesar salad.

"You feeling okay?" He squinted and studied her face. She was a younger, trimmer version of her mother—pretty, in a quiet way, with brownish hair and a shy smile. She was paler than usual, even for her fair skin.

"I'm fine, thanks. Just a little tired after last night." She set down her fork, dabbed her mouth with a napkin, and sipped water.

"Yeah. We all missed our beauty sleep." He didn't feel one bit tired. The tour, followed by a day at Goldview School, shot energy through his system like a vigorous workout. The impact of impromptu activities in little Goldview surprised him. Or was a certain woman responsible for the boost in his spirits?

"Did you have fun?" Shauna smothered a yawn.

"Sure did. Jill and I both had a good time." He probably shouldn't speak for Jill, but if he studied hard, he read amusement in her eyes, peeking out behind her tight expression. He swooped a fry through ketchup, shoved it into his mouth, and chased it with a huge bite of burger.

"I'm glad." Shauna slid away her bowl. "I'm too tired to eat right now."

"I'll inhale my food and let you go. Hey, does Jill play a sport? Or like yoga or any kind of activity?"

Shauna shrugged. "She walks Georgia. Why do you ask?"

Her mannerisms reminded him of Jill. "Exercise is good for a person. After school, I dropped by her place—Cody once pointed out the house where you grew up. I invited her out to snowshoe. Nola let me borrow two pairs from the school." He shrugged and mopped his plate with the last bite of burger. "She declined and frowned like I asked her to take a polar plunge."

A hot rush of rejection had travelled up his spine and grabbed the back of his neck. The feeling was all too familiar. He had been a chubby kid who strove to fit in but never quite did. Along the way, his smart mouth covered his pain and insecurity, but finally, after a bad marriage and sticky divorce, he discovered the benefits of exercise.

He related to the way Jill must feel. He wouldn't mention to Shauna the way Jill tugged down her sweater like she wanted to disappear behind a curtain. She carried a few extra pounds but didn't need to feel ashamed of her body. He'd been in the same place and come out the other side, but not without a lot of hard work and commitment.

"I'm not surprised she refused, but if you try again,

good luck." Shauna glanced over her shoulder and smiled at Cody.

Wearing a black hairnet and orange apron, Cody bustled to their table, bent, and kissed Shauna. "Hey, honey. Sorry, I'm so busy I can't stop. Hope your food was good, Dad. Like I said, while you teach at the school here, feel free to bunk at our place."

"Thanks, Code. Food's great as usual. At the show of affection between his son and daughter-in-law, he scrunched his napkin. Envy twisted like a wine corkscrew in his chest. As a single, he'd kissed a few women, but he still hadn't clicked with the right one. Nobody uncovered the real him or lit a fire. His looks and personality should attract a winner, but nope. Not so far. He didn't understand any of the string of women, either.

"Not hungry, honey?" Cody rubbed a hand along Shauna's shoulders.

"I ate a little. It was good." She smiled up at Cody. "Thank you."

"You're welcome, honey." Cody's gaze lingered on Shauna, and then he straightened the napkin dispenser and gathered dishes. "Make yourself at home, Dad. The spare bedroom downstairs is all yours."

"Thanks for putting me up. Or should I say putting up with me?" Jack chuckled and slurped the rest of his cola. "Right after dinner, I plan to drive home and pick up a few things. I'll return to your place in a couple of hours."

He sized up Cody and Shauna. The chemistry between them sizzled. Lucky kids. Someday, he'd find the right woman…or had he found her already?

Chapter 10

A valentine joke from one of Jill's students: What did the boy octopus say to the girl octopus?

I want to hold your hand, hand, hand, hand, hand, hand, hand, hand.

*****

After school on Friday, Jill tidied her classroom and sorted assignments to mark. As the hallways cleared, laughter and chatter faded to peaceful quiet. The kids' watercolor landscapes hung in neat, pastel rows on the bulletin board at the side. She'd wrap up within a few minutes and head home to her new regime—a brisk outing followed by a low-calorie dinner. *Goodbye, sluggish Jill. Hello, fitter Jill of the past.*

Pausing, she checked her phone for messages.

—*Jack likes you. A lot!*—

Texting was a way of life, but Jill still wasn't accustomed to the way Shauna jumped into a conversation without a hello. Tapping a quick response, Jill shook her head and smiled. Her fingers quivered.

—*Hi, Shauna. How was your day?*—

—*Did you hear me? LOL*—

—*Unfortunately. LOL*—

Jill shook her head at Shauna's teasing.

—*Give the poor guy a break. He's lonely. Go on another date.*—

—The tour was not a date.—

Jill backed up her cursor and changed the word *not* to all capital letters.

—Are you sure?—

Shauna added a winking face emoji.

Jill ignored the bait.

—Want to join me for tea this evening?—

Jill scanned the classroom for anything left to tidy before she left.

—Thanks, Momsy, but maybe tomorrow. I'm pretty tired.—

—Okay. Have a good rest. TTYS. XO—

—Invite Jack instead!—

Still smiling at Shauna's final quip, Jill set down her phone. At a tap on the open door, she glanced up. "Hi, Nola." The principal seldom popped in, especially at home time.

"Do you have a minute?" Nola strode toward Jill's desk at the front and plunked on a table opposite.

"Of course." Even at the end of a busy day, Nola's sleek hair remained in place, and her black pantsuit and violet blouse stayed wrinkle free. Jill sank into her chair and brushed a stray hair off her cheek. She adjusted the hem of her chocolate-brown sweater over the waistband of her matching, tweedy pants. Was Nola here to discuss a behavioral issue? Feedback from a disgruntled parent? The winter carnival? Jill couldn't guess, so she waited.

"I trust your judgment and wanted to consult you on a staffing decision." Nola gripped the table on either side of her legs and leaned forward.

The clank of the caretaker's wash bucket and a faint waft of lemon-scented cleaner drifted from the hallway into the classroom.

"Sure." Jill straightened, nodded, and smiled. She had worked with Nola for years and knew the principal valued her opinions, but hearing praise still mattered. Then, instantly, her arms prickled like her cotton sweater switched to scratchy wool. Nola was about to ask her about…

"Jack Ryan. I'd like to offer him a contract to fill the maternity leave. You know him well. Do you agree he fits with our school team?" Nola kept her gaze on Jill.

"Uh…" Jack pulsed with energy. He cared about the students. He promoted healthy living. Although he was a bit boastful and persistent for her taste, he meant well. She wouldn't dare give him a thumbs-down. "He shows a lot of the qualities the school needs."

"You sound hesitant." Nola studied Jill's expression.

"I didn't mean…" Jill shook her head and folded her hands on her desk.

"If you have concerns, please, tell me." Nola crossed her legs. "Then I'll make one request."

Jill opened and shut her mouth. She couldn't recommend against hiring him just because he liked her and continually suggested more time together. When her heart thumped at his attention, how could she possibly blackball him? She didn't need to admit to the complications of new feelings, did she? Nola didn't need to know excitement bounced like a basketball in her stomach. Jill swallowed. "I can't think of any reason not to offer him the job."

"Thank you. I'm glad to hear you have no concerns." She paused. "I sense you and Jack are close." Nola raised her hands and formed air quotation marks around the word close. She smiled and winked.

Jill wanted to slap her hands over her burning cheeks, but she released the tight grip of her interwoven fingers, forced a laugh, and waved away a palm. "We're not dating, if that's what you mean." Of course, Nola had observed them together on the tour and the way they interacted at school. Based on the superficial evidence, an outsider might suspect Jack was her guy. But really…

"Don't worry, Jill. You don't have to discuss your love life." Nola shifted and uncrossed her legs. "All I ask is you keep romance away from school. It won't be the first relationship between coworkers. Did I ever tell you I met Doug at my first teaching post?" She didn't wait for a response. "But I'm sure you can appreciate I don't want anything to interfere with the job."

"Of course." Jill nodded. "But we're not…"

"Things change." Nola hopped off the table. "You never know."

Knees slightly unsteady, Jill rose opposite Nola. "We'll see if you're right, but I doubt it." Her face still tingled with warmth. Was Nola especially perceptive, or did she see obvious signs of smouldering attraction?

"Don't tell Jack, but I'll call him tonight to offer him the job. Have a good evening, Jill." Nola breezed out of the room.

Breathing a lingering trace of Nola's rose-scented cologne, Jill spread her arms, tipped back her head, and rotated until she dizzied. She ran her hands up the sides of her ample hips and threw them in the air like she cheered for a touchdown by her favorite football team. Now that she exercised more, she didn't hate her body quite so much.

"Score a goal?" Jack stuck his head around the doorframe and, without an invitation, marched into the room.

Jill dropped her hands and relaxed her grin into a demure smile. Jack caught her off guard again. "I needed a good stretch. Yoga is healthy, right, Mr. Fitness?" She lilted her voice to take any bite out of her words. She hardly understood her impromptu cheer, but she sure didn't want him to suspect it had anything to do with him."

"Thanks." He puffed out his chest. "The title suits me. So...ready to cross-country ski?"

"Pardon me? You mean right now? I don't even ski." She plunked hands on hips. He never gave up. She would get fit her own way and, definitely, not by bowing to his idea of a good time.

He strolled to a spot less than a meter away and planted himself opposite her.

Jack hovered so close she breathed his clean scent, as fresh as prairie air after a rain. Hands in the front pockets of his black jeans, he sent a clear message he was in no rush to leave.

"Okay. We can skate instead."

"Thanks, but not today." She glanced down and organized papers. Her breath quickened, and she wavered slightly off balance. She liked skating. In fact, years ago, she even figure skated, and when Shauna was a pre-schooler, Jill held her hand and glided over the ice. But now, she was so rusty she might wobble like a beginner. Maybe someday she'd lace up her old skates, but she'd need a private practice session before she appeared in public. Anticipation whirled like a skating spin in her heart.

"All right." He yanked his hands out of his jeans pockets and pumped both fists. "Here's my final offer."

Jill raised her eyebrows and took a deep, calming breath. "What now?" Would she relent or stand firm?

"I'll join you to walk your dog."

Jill couldn't argue she didn't have the time or the inclination. After school, she always exercised Georgia. While she had often considered the excursion just one more chore, now she viewed it as a healthy part of her day. She glanced out the classroom windows and blinked at the light glinting off snowbanks. Bundled up in warm clothes, she'd enjoy the cold air and moderate exercise. She tugged at the bottom of her sweater and smoothed it over her stomach. As long as he didn't set too fast a pace, Jack's company might be okay. "Do I have a choice?" He wasn't the only one who could tease.

"Nope, but you won't be sorry." Jack grinned. "I'll meet you at your place in half an hour." He spun and loped out the door.

A simple stroll with her dog did not count as a date. Pulse jumping, Jill gathered her things and slid her marking homework into a tote bag. Wait until Audrey heard the latest.

Chapter 11

Wisdom from Jill and Audrey's mom: Love isn't complicated, but people are.

****

A few days later, Jill trudged over snowbanks to the station in the school yard where she'd supervise the snowball toss at the winter carnival. She'd make the best of her assigned activity, even though it wasn't her first choice. She'd stepped up her exercise but couldn't totally reform overnight. Serving hot chocolate with fluffy marshmallows was more her speed.

Her heart pattered from the combination of exertion and Jack's presence in his chunky boots and navy parka. Since the tour, he had sought out her company every single day, and her feelings rode a rollercoaster at the sudden change in her routine. Sometimes he made her laugh, but just as often, his wisecracks fell flat. If he just relaxed and didn't try so hard to amuse everybody, he'd appeal to people a lot more.

"Jack and Jill went up the hill..." Climbing a slight incline, Jack smacked together his hands in leathery mitts and quoted the nursery rhyme. "Like I told Merilee, see how we belong together."

"Shhh." Smothering a laugh, Jill glanced side to side and over her shoulder to make sure no kids were close enough to hear. Teachers' first names were strictly off limits, and so was romance in the school yard. As much as possible, she'd keep her distance, just like Nola expected.

The evening Nola called to offer Jack a continuing contract, he had shared the news within minutes.

"Hi, Jill. I didn't know who else to call." Jack cleared his throat. "Cody's at the restaurant, and Shauna's napping."

The excitement in his voice bubbled out of her phone. "Do you have good news?" After her conversation with Nola, she guessed the cause of his elation, but she feigned curiosity. Instead of flopping on the couch to talk like her natural inclination, she paced in a circle from the kitchen through the living room and back. Striding, maybe she could escape the avalanche of feelings that threatened to bury her.

Now Jack was officially her coworker, and she would see him every weekday. She would discuss students' progress, bump into him in the hallway, and eat in the same staff room. If she visited the gym at lunchtime, she'd encounter him, for sure. Oddly, why didn't she mind? In just a few days, how could she have changed her opinion so drastically?

"Nope. It's *great* news!" Jack raised his voice. "Nola hired me to fill in for the next year."

"Congratulations and welcome aboard." Jill paused. What else could she say? She took her time to word a genuine response. "You'll do well, and when you get to know the other teachers, you'll find them friendly and supportive."

"Thanks, Jill. I mean it. Maybe we can get together and celebrate. You can toast me...clink a glass of champagne or two."

"Uh…" Why did he continually leave her speechless? "At the very least, I'll raise my coffee mug in the staff room." With nothing else to say, she had ended the call and splashed cold water on her face.

Now, in the school yard, the snow crunched under her knee-high boots, and the sun beamed overhead like a spotlight on the day. As the forecast promised, temperatures moderated just in time to spend a comfortable half day outside immersed in fun, winter activities. Bending and scooping a handful of snow, she formed it into a ball, threw it into the air, and let it splat in the space between her and Jack. The sticky consistency was ideal for snowballs and snowmen.

"You're lucky you didn't hit me. I throw a mean curveball." Jack grinned, grabbed his own handful, and flung it far ahead.

"Nice throw, Mr. Ryan." Eli romped along with a group of other boys from Jill's class.

Clearly mischievous and confident, Eli was the tall, blond ringleader of the grade five boys, and Jill kept a close watch on his behavior. Today he wore a gray jacket with his curly hair shoved under a black, knitted beanie.

"Thanks. Let's see yours." Jack pointed a fat mitt at Eli.

"I bet I can throw mine farther." Eli grinned and demonstrated.

"Impressive. Now let's see how you all do with a target." Jack spun and tromped backward, facing the rest of the grade fives.

Around the kids, Jack's brash manner faded, and he transformed into a fun, yet firm, teacher and role model. He related well to the class, especially the rowdy boys.

The group jostled their way to the wooden snowman structure parent volunteers set up earlier. The game was to throw snowballs through holes in the figure's mouth and stomach.

Jill scanned the field for stragglers, and sure enough, Oscar traipsed alone, far behind the rest. Even from a distance, Jill could tell he puffed from the exertion of dragging his heavy body through the snow. About to backtrack to encourage him, she felt a hand brush her arm.

"I'll go." Jack left her with the rest of the kids and headed in long strides toward Oscar.

Sudden warmth tingled into Jill's chest. Maybe she should listen to Audrey's advice and open her heart to Jack. Audrey had urged Merilee to pursue a romance with Ross, and now, they both basked in the glow of true love. First Audrey, then Nola, and even Shauna teased her about Jack, so they must sense obvious chemistry. Clearly, behind Jack's outer facade lived a sensitive guy who did the right thing. Combined with his clean-cut, good looks and the fact he overlooked her round hips, how could she resist?

****

Before he backtracked to check on Oscar, Jack caught a glimpse of Jill's quick smile. Her wrinkled forehead, peeking under the brim of her brown, woolen hat, relaxed a bit. He demonstrated his concern, and she approved. Jack tromped back to meet Oscar. "Hey, bud, how are you doing? The trek to the first station is a bit of a workout. Are you excited about the carnival?"

"Not really." Oscar puffed and wheezed.

"No? How come?" Maybe Jack could convince

Oscar to open up. He glanced at the boy's cheeks. They were bright red, probably more from exertion than from the fresh air. An overweight kid struggled to do physical things like other boys and girls. He remembered all too well. A kid who was different stuck out. A kid who didn't fit in attracted teasing…and worse, bullying. Painful memories burned in Jack's throat. Oscar needed his encouragement. He needed someone who cared enough to help.

Oscar shrugged. "I like math and stuff better."

"Oh. Any other reason?"

Silent except for his heavy breathing, Oscar struggled along. "I'm not good at throwing and running. The other kids…they're all friends…"

"Must be tough." Jack lowered his voice so the other kids wouldn't hear. Life could be difficult without someone to listen—even for an adult. "Just do your best today. We can talk more later. Okay?"

Oscar nodded, and at the edge of the milling group, he planted his feet and heaved breaths.

Organizing rows for the activity, Jill called instructions and motioned with her arms.

For an instant, Jack glued his gaze onto her face. In the cold air, her breath formed light, white wisps. Then he jerked his attention to a huddle of loud boys.

Backing away from Oscar, Eli laughed and pointed.

The rest of the group gawked and chuckled at the scene.

Arms flailing, Oscar sprawled flat on his back.

A hot burst of anger rushed from Jack's shoulders to his temples. With all the noise and jostling, he didn't catch exactly what happened, but he guessed. In two long strides, he reached Oscar and extended a hand to hoist him upright. He'd confer with Jill later on how best to address the other boys' bullying behavior. "Get in line. Now." Jack glared at the group. "And keep your arms and legs to yourself."

Jill gaped at the disturbance and dropped her arms to her sides.

"Ms. Meyers, I need to consult you." Jack called Jill by the formal name the kids used and crunched away from the group. Lowering his voice, he shared his idea and confirmed she agreed. Still seething at the mistreatment of Oscar, he listened to Jill's instructions.

"We need someone to count and record points." She scanned the group. "Oscar, would you like to be the scorekeeper?"

Oscar breathed out hard and nodded.

Jill motioned the boy forward and, for an instant, met Jack's gaze.

He caught her slight nod and unspoken message of thanks. Did he even detect a glint of admiration? He only did the right thing for a kid who needed support, but Jill's approval helped relax his tight shoulders.

Just as the group's time wrapped up at the snowball toss, Nola drifted by to check on logistics and cheer on the kids. "Everything going well?" She glanced from Jill to Jack.

"Mostly. While I point the kids to the next station, you can fill her in, Jack." Jill motioned for everyone to follow.

Standing next to the principal, he waited until no one could overhear. Even outside, Nola dressed in a sleek, put-together way. Her gray jacket and matching hat blended like paint samples with the silvery color of her hair. The smell of her rose perfume floated in sharp contrast with the clean scent of winter. "Some of the boys knocked over Oscar. Poor kid. I gather he struggles." Jack shook his head. "I don't allow any kind of bullying, even if it's labelled goofing off. Jill and I agreed we'll deal with the culprits back in the classroom."

"Thanks for the update." Nola narrowed her eyes. "I agree. Bullies don't belong at Goldview School. I'll ask the other teachers and volunteers to keep a close watch." She inhaled a deep breath and smiled. "What a beautiful day! Have fun." Then she scooted off to the next activity, leaving Jack and Jill to await the next group.

"Okay." Jill faced Jack.

"Okay, what?" Jack studied her face. She was cute with her round, pink cheeks and wide, amber eyes. Bright sunshine and fresh air flattered her.

"I'll join you to skate." She blinked and tilted her head.

"Because you can't resist me." He smirked and shoved his thumbs into his chest.

"Ha ha. Do you really think so? Maybe I just like to skate. Now shhh." She raised a gloved finger to her lips. "Here comes the next batch."

A silent cheer exploded in Jack's chest. She liked him. She wanted to spend more time with him. From the outside, she looked and acted nothing like the women he chased in the past. But more and more, she glowed with attractive qualities, inside and out. His heart pumped like he just ran a race and won first prize. Finally, had he found a special someone?

Chapter 12

Advice from Jill and Audrey's mom: "Always follow your heart, but remember to bring along your brain."

****

After school, Jill popped into Goldview Gifts to tell Audrey the latest development with Jack. Her stomach fluttered with more butterflies than a flower garden. She never imagined resolving to get fit and getting stranded on a Sweetheart Tour could lead to...was it genuine romance?

Inside, she paused to drink in the sights, scents, and sounds. Audrey decorated for every new season and special occasion, and this month, the store was a pink, red, and white wonderland of hearts, snowflakes, and roses. Tiny white lights framed the large, front window, and figurines of snowmen and Cupids decorated the shelves, interspersed among glassware, ornaments, and jewellery. The scents of rose and jasmine meandered along the cramped aisles, and soft love songs floated overhead.

Scanning for Audrey, she landed her gaze on a woman bustling toward the door.

Merilee Mills, the tour host and Audrey's best friend, approached. "Hello, Jill. How nice to see you again. I just finished my visit with your sister." She flashed a wide smile and clasped her hands in front of her chest. "Your turn now."

"Oh, good. I timed my visit right." Jill smiled and shifted. Normally, Merilee's trim figure, blondish hair, and pretty features made Jill feel a bit mousy, but she gathered from Audrey that Merilee didn't have a conceited bone in her body. Merilee had long ago given up on romance until she hired Ross as her tour bus driver. Even though Jill didn't share similar looks or pizzazz, she admitted the story gave her hope.

"How did you enjoy the tour, aside from the minor weather glitch?" Merilee touched Jill's arm. "The next day, I bet you were exhausted at school." Purse dangling from one arm, she flung up her palms. "You can be honest with me. I want to keep all my guests happy, so I need your feedback. I tell my sweetie, Ross, to keep his ears open, too. Don't you agree we're a perfect team?" She tilted her head and giggled. "When I hired him, I never dreamt I'd fall in love."

Jill opened and closed her mouth and waited for Merilee to take a breath. Definitely, Merilee needed Audrey's steady and calming influence. Overhead, pretty, glass bumblebee mobiles dangled messages like *Bee Mine* and *You're My Honey*.

"Anyway, what did you think?" Merilee studied Jill's face. "I noticed you and Jack enjoyed each other's company."

At the innuendo in Merilee's bubbly comment, Jill swallowed. "You planned a wonderful evening. It was really lovely. Even getting stranded added fun." She smiled and slapped a hand over her chest. The morning after, she wouldn't have given the tour such a glowing report, but now she better understood—and appreciated—the true Jack, and the whole memory glowed like a rosy sunrise.

"I'm so glad to hear, Jill. Thank you for the compliment, and please, tell all your friends. You must know a lot of teachers who could use some romance in their lives." Merilee rolled onto her toes. "I had no idea you dated Jack Ryan. You and your daughter must have similar taste in men." She clapped together her hands. "Well, I better run and leave you with Audrey. Ta-ta." She blew an air kiss.

Should Jill correct her and insist the Sweetheart Tour wasn't an actual date? Or did Merilee foreshadow things to come? The idea Jill found ludicrous just ten days ago was now an exciting possibility.

"What a nice surprise." Audrey wove from the sales desk at the back. "First, Merilee, and now, you. Will you come to the back for herbal tea? I just made a pot."

As always, Audrey shone a warm expression and peered from behind her trademark tortoiseshell glasses. In a rare change of wardrobe color scheme, she wore a pale-pink sweater with the same shade of pants. Maybe she dressed to match her décor.

Without waiting for an answer, Audrey motioned to follow, led Jill to the combined stockroom and coffee area, and poured mugs of steaming tea.

The flowery scents from the store faded away, replaced by the aroma of orange spice. How many times had Jill sought Audrey's advice at this table? She settled on a chair, slipped off her jacket, and warmed her hands around the mug.

"Well?" Audrey sipped tea and peeked over the rim. "I can't wait to hear your news."

"You were right to tell me to give Jack a chance."

Audrey would tease, but Jill didn't mind.

"I won't say I told you so." Audrey smiled and set down her mug.

"At school, I discovered he hides genuine substance behind his obsession with fitness and his questionable sense of humor." Jill laughed and wrinkled her nose.

Audrey nodded. "Go on."

"I really can't avoid him, so why fight it? I joined him for a few brisk walks, and now, I invited him to skate. Originally, he suggested the idea, and I declined, but then I listened to my heart."

"Go for it. I'm proud of your big flip-flop. I helped Merilee find the ideal guy, and you are my next project." Smiling, Audrey lifted her mug in a mock toast. "Here's to love. What changed your mind?"

"A bully."

"A bully?" Audrey raised her eyebrows.

"Oscar, one of the boys in my class, is overweight and a constant target of the cool boys' mean tricks, despite my efforts to teach kindness and to discipline them. Right away, Jack singled out Oscar and offered support." Jill's insides warmed, even without another sip of tea. "His compassion touched me. I admire his care and concern for the students, even though I need to excuse parts of his brash exterior. Nobody's perfect."

"You sure don't need to overlook his appearance." Laughing, Audrey tilted forward and brushed Jill's forearm.

Blushing, Jill clutched her mug and stared at the rising steam. "True. I didn't expect a guy like him to show any interest, but I won't complain."

"He sees you as an intelligent, nice, attractive

woman, which doesn't surprise me in the least. Give yourself the credit you deserve. Remember, you just said nobody's perfect."

"Thanks for your vote of confidence." Audrey had always been her biggest cheerleader. Jill's thighs bulged over the edges of the chair, and she squelched a cringe. Shifting, she adjusted her sweater and sucked in her stomach. She would continue to tone her body, but even now, she would accept herself—lumps, rolls, and all.

"Soon we can double date. Won't we have fun?" Audrey widened her eyes. "Let me know when you want to invite him to dinner at our place."

Just then, a jingle of the bell on the front door announced the arrival of a customer. "That sound is my cue to leave." Smiling, Jill jumped up and zipped her jacket. "Thanks for tea…and the confidence boost."

"Enjoy your evening." Audrey hustled ahead of Jill into the retail area of the shop.

Jill exited into a cold breeze that nipped her cheeks and nose. Taking deep breaths, she hurried along a snowy sidewalk past the eclectic storefronts of Omar's Foods, Dr. MacMillan's office, and Prairie Hair. Her spirits leapt so high she practically soared toward home. She raised a hand at a neighbor who drove by and greeted a familiar-looking passerby. Even in the dead of winter, Goldview enveloped her in cozy, familiar surroundings. Life here was safe and predictable…at least, until now. Would an official date with the new teacher in town flip everything upside down?

****

"After dinner, I'm going skating with your mom." Jack glanced up from his beef stew at Cody and

Shauna's kitchen table. Cody supervised the dinner rush at Burger Town, so Jack dined with Shauna, which was a perfect opportunity to enlist her support. The aromas of onion and garlic combined with rich, beefy gravy filled the room, and his stomach rumbled.

"My mom agreed to go skating?" Shauna stopped chewing. "I can't believe she listened."

Jack loaded his fork with potatoes. "Yum. You cook almost as well as your husband." Shauna could take a joke. The chrome table, matching chairs, and square canister set, all bright red, were a throwback to his childhood home, just like the comfort food on his plate.

"Ha ha, Jack. Be careful, or we'll evict you." Fork poised, she ran her gaze over his expression.

"Did you tell your mom to abandon the couch?" Just talking about Jill increased Jack's heartrate. Shauna was an ally who could help sway Jill to give him a chance.

"I told her to give you a break and go on a date."

Jack snorted. "You're responsible? I assumed my charming personality changed her mind." He dragged a bun and mopped gravy. Glancing at Shauna across the table, he pictured a young, more vivid version of Jill. Her gold sweater highlighted the flecks in her unlined, brown eyes. Youth always faded, but he still spotted remnants in Jill. A fitter body—not that he minded her generous curves—would peel away years. "How could she resist?" He flicked his eyebrows.

Shauna grimaced and shook her head.

Jack chuckled. She gave him the exact reaction he invited with his joking conceit. Shauna was a fun, spunky match for Cody. As a young, married couple, they had already figured out love better than he ever experienced.

"Excuse me, Jack." She set down her fork and retrieved her phone out of a pocket. "I need to text Mom right this minute." She whisked over the keypad with both thumbs, smiled, and set aside the phone.

Jack filled his mouth with potato and carrot chunks and savored the earthy flavor. A long time ago, he learned the slower he chewed, the more time he gave his brain to signal he was full. "What did you say?" A second helping would taste great but wouldn't help his stomach stay flat.

"I said, 'Way to follow my advice!'" Shauna buttered a bun.

A sharp ting sent a message alert. Jill must have sent a quick reply.

Shauna scanned the message. "Mom said, 'I trust your advice. Most of the time. LOL. What do you mean?'" Shauna keyed a reply and glanced up. "I just wrote, 'Your date with Jack. He says he's one heck of a guy.'"

"It's true." Jack tapped a fist on the table. On the inside, he didn't feel nearly as self-assured, but his daughter-in-law probably didn't suspect. "You didn't really make up that quote, did you?"

"Yep. Just to get her more excited about your evening." Shauna speared a bite of meat.

"Is it possible?" Jack matched Shauna's light banter, and hope surged in a hot rush from his torso to his limbs. At another ping, he held his breath.

Shauna scanned the screen. Laughing, she typed with her thumbs.

Jill must have sent a witty reply. "Well?" Jack

waited for Shauna to share.

"She said, 'Tell Jack to prove it! And Shauna, if you still lived at home, I'd ground you for interfering in my social life.'"

Jill might be an introvert, but she wasn't a pushover. He couldn't wait to circle the ice rink and see her face lit by moonlight and stars.

Chapter 13

SASK radio announcer: My buddy promised his girlfriend a diamond for Valentine's Day.

He took her to a ballgame.

****

The evening shone bright, and the promise of a stronger connection with Jack tingled all the way to the tips of Jill's fingers and toes. "Don't expect too much." Seated on a wooden bench, Jill dove forward and laced her skates. "When I was young, I figure skated, but I haven't attempted anything fancy since Shauna was about twelve." In thick clothing, her stomach and legs were like sausages stuffed into casing, but she refused to let her shape ruin her fun. One day at a time, she'd transform.

She sniffed the cold air scented with the smoky smell of a wood fireplace burning somewhere in the neighborhood. The small, oval rink hid within a border of snowbanks and evergreens like a picture from a Christmas card. White lights draped like sparkly ribbons along the edges, and overhead, a clear sky displayed a shiny moon and a canopy of stars. The romantic setting sent her stomach into a flutter.

"Skating is like riding a bike. You never forget how." With a puffy, black mitt, Jack tapped her knee.

She barely sensed his touch through her ski pants, layered over thick leggings, but her whole body warmed. Attraction was nothing like riding a bike. She remembered the feeling, but it still threw her way off balance. "Tell my knees they better behave." She straightened and glanced at Jack. The shadowy light didn't obscure his piercing, blue eyes or mischievous, wide grin. Only their voices broke the silence.

"Do your knees like being told what to do any better than the rest of you?" Chuckling, he tied his second skate and jumped to his feet. Bundled in a navy parka, he tugged a black, knitted hat lower over his forehead.

What do you mean?" She joined him in laughter and, with feet planted apart, stood without a wobble. Did he sense she needed to prove she was independent and capable? She might change but on her own terms. "I listen to good advice...sometimes. In a minute, I'll see whether I should have listened to my own counsel to practice before I appeared in public." With a tentative push, she glided away from the bench.

"Nice start." Jack zipped ahead and flipped backward to face her.

"I'm not worried." Jill held out her arms for balance and stroked from one foot to the other. "If I fall, you'll catch me." Filling her lungs with frosty air, she hardly recognized the flirtatious tone of her own voice. Jack affected her in surprising ways, but heaven forbid he should actually need to break her fall. She still packed a significant amount of weight; yet, she wouldn't let her physical condition put a damper on the evening. On the Sweetheart Tour, she boogied all right on the dance floor, and her old skills reappeared, so why not on the ice? Whether Jack realized or not, she already headed toward a fitter life.

"You bet." Jack circled her with choppy crossovers. "Whatever you need, let me know."

"You make me dizzy with your whizzing around." Did she whirl inside because of his motion or something else? A typical evening at home with Georgia was so much more predictable than venturing onto a patch of ice with a man who threw confusion into her heart. An official date with her daughter's father-in-law didn't make sense.

Maybe she shouldn't have accepted Jack's invitation. Alone in dark, romantic surroundings, anything could happen. After her broken marriage, she still needed to prove she functioned just fine without Wes. She would rediscover her old self without interference or coaching from a man. But right now, crazy feelings danced around sensible thoughts, and they intermingled into an exciting, yet unsettling, party in her stomach. Her heartbeat quickened. Ever since she rode the tour bus next to Jack, she didn't understand her reactions to anything. How could one evening as a forced companion and one week as a skeptical co-worker make such a difference in her ability to reason?

"If you're ready, let's go." Jack quit circling, braked, and then glided forward.

Jill crackled over the ice to his side. She relaxed her stiff knees and trusted they would support her weight. Picking up speed, she tasted the carefree rush of cold air on her face. Her toe picks scratched and caught bits of ice. Jack was right. Muscle memory took over, and her old skills chased away any lingering hesitation. Exhilaration filled her with such light, buoyant optimism she could float.

"Not bad. You skate almost as well as me."

Throwing a grin over his shoulder, Jack zigzagged ahead then skidded to a stop and sent a fluffy shower of snow off his blades.

"And you're almost as modest as me." Jill lengthened her stride and passed him. "Just wait until you really see me in action." His chuckle drifted through the frosty, evening air. The cool temperature contrasted with the warm glow in her chest...lit by...could Jack really be responsible?

Her heartrate dipped and sped like it wore its own pair of skates. Sometimes Jack acted overly confident and even conceited about his appearance and fitness, but underneath his cocky comments and know-it-all expression, she sensed uncertainty. He should quit trying so hard to prove his worth. Already, he was plenty good enough.

Laughing and breathing in quick bursts, Jill accelerated and glanced over her shoulder in time to see Jack leap forward, lose his balance, and land on his side. "Nice splat. Are you hurt?" She jammed in a toe pick, stopped, and spun backward. His crumpled expression disappeared behind a grin. In the shimmering light, she couldn't tell whether his eyes reflected humor or embarrassment.

"You swept me off my feet." Jack bounced up and brushed ice shavings off his pants.

"I have that effect on men." She laughed and trusted the dim lighting to cover her blush. Why did she say something flirtatious that wasn't even true? Around Jack, she was a woman she didn't recognize. With a giant thrust, she nabbed a head start and snapped over tiny bumps on the ice surface.

"Hey, wait." Jack soon swooped beside her.

"Watch this." Jill lowered into a squat and extended one leg. Her pants strained at the waist and across her bottom but didn't tear, thank goodness.

"Impressive. What do you call that maneuver?"

"Shoot the Duck." She wobbled, drew in her leg, and straightened. "It was one of my signature moves. Try it."

"Here goes." He bent partway, groaned, and stood. "Or not."

"Mr. Fit is not Mr. Flexible." Jill laughed and spun once. "Maybe if you practice, you'll do better next time." She could tease, too. To get a head start, she hopped and took off but couldn't outskate him for long.

Circling the rink, she stretched her free leg and arced toward and then away from Jack. Her bulk floated away, and confidence expanded in her chest like a balloon that would never pop. She soared as alive and free as the old, energetic Jill. Goodbye to the tired woman who crumpled on the couch with potato chips to comfort her while she coped with the disappointments and adjustments of a failed marriage. Intermission from regular, active life was over.

For a few moments, only the crisp, cutting sounds of their blades broke the still, silent air.

"Will you—"

"I wish—" Hearing Jack speak at the same moment, Jill slowed and curved side to side.

"Ladies first." Jack swung forward an arm.

"I wish every night could be this beautiful." She glanced at the starry sky. Did it twinkle the promise of happy days to follow?

"In my amazing presence?" He stuck a thumb in his chest.

"I mean...I don't know what I mean. What were you about to say?" She lowered her gaze to his profile and absorbed the cold, peaceful air brushing her cheeks.

"Will you allow me to hold your hand?" He gave a slight bow and extended an arm

The bold man disappeared, replaced by a hesitant gentleman. At the same time, she melted from a mature woman into a fluttery teen. Passing fragrant evergreens, she couldn't quite take a full breath. Would she? Should she?" Under her blades, the ice snapped. Her mouth dried so she couldn't speak, so she nodded and held out a hand.

He enveloped it with his black mitts. "Just a sec." He let go and yanked off a mitt. Then he tugged off one of hers and squeezed her bare hand. "Much better. Skin on skin."

His palm and fingers radiated warmth, and she soaked in the pleasurable sensation like a soothing bath. Circuiting the rink, she scanned the wide backdrop of sky and the white blanket below. Gliding along, she memorized every detail—the smooth, firm texture of Jack's hand, the crunch of blades over ice, tree branches spread with snow like icing, white puffs of air, and the smell of clean air scented by pine. Town lights peeked through trees, and white smoke rose from chimneys.

"Are you cold?" Slowing, he scraped to a stop, released his hold, and returned her mitt.

"Only my tingly fingers and icicle nose." She might be chilly on the outside but not on the inside. With heat jumping like a forest fire from her middle to every part of her body, she hardly needed a winter jacket. Jack had no idea where her mind skated. "With my mitt on again, I'll be fine. I'm not ready to quit yet."

"Me either." He replaced his mitt, grasped her hand, and shoved off, towing her like a wagon.

"Thank you, Jack."

"For the free ride?" He laughed and swerved side to side.

"Whoa. I feel like I'm at an amusement park." She eased her toes inward to slow the ride.

"You're on your own." He laughed, released his hold, and jumped backward to face her. "Thank you for what? Charming you as always?"

"For being kind to Oscar." She detected the waver in her voice, maybe caused by bumping over an uneven patch but more likely from compassion. Oscar needed all the support he could get. "You understood the first day you taught here and helped him find his missing boot. Then today, you rescued him from the class bullies."

"Been there. Done that," Jack murmured.

"Oh?" What did he mean? Did he refer to the many times he helped other kids or to personal experience? With a sudden crackle, she caught a blade edge, wobbled, and regained her balance.

"I was the fat kid who the other kids terrorized. To survive, I cracked bad jokes and tossed out smart comments." He shrugged. "Ten years ago, my divorce shook me into a big change. I worked out, lost fifty pounds, and attended a support group. I needed to process a whack of rejection and build confidence."

Jill swallowed and slowed. Cold seeped through her jacket and wound around her like a spool of icy thread. No wonder he flaunted his fit body and wisecracked his way through social situations. He didn't mean to offend, but somehow, he needed to cover deep-rooted feelings of inferiority.

Curving, he cleared his throat. "I don't usually spill my secrets."

"Don't worry. They're safe here." She inhaled a deep breath, hugged her arms over her chest, and sealed them inside. He trusted her, and her bulky shape didn't matter.

"I know." Switching to crossovers and motioning to follow, he cleared his throat.

The spell broken, Jill accelerated and demonstrated slightly shaky crossovers in his wake.

In a smooth motion, he switched directions and carved a giant eight.

Puffing so hard her jacket rustled under her chin, Jill nearly kept pace. She wouldn't let him see she struggled to keep up. The painful image of Oscar lagging behind his classmates flashed to mind. As she boosted her activity level, exercise would get easier, but she didn't need a pep talk from Jack. Muscles burning, she forced strong, steady strokes. Just when her legs couldn't stand the punishment any longer, she traced his slowing motion and practically shouted her relief.

Jack drew his feet together, swooped toward the bench where they started, and plopped down. "Whew. Even this fit bod gets tired sometimes."

About to join him, Jill stiffened. Did she really belong next to a guy obsessed with exercise and appearance? She lowered herself onto the bench and silently cursed the roll that bulged over the waistband of her ski pants. She breathed out in a whoosh, and the snap popped open. Why now? She rolled her eyes, but at least, Jack couldn't see the gap under her jacket.

The frozen bench sent a chill through her ski pants and into her bones, and she shivered. The rhythm of her breathing intermingled with Jack's, and puffs of wispy, white clouds drifted from their mouths. Bending forward, she jerked her laces undone and removed her skates. Even in jest, he sounded like a bit of a braggart and somebody she'd typically avoid. When he didn't show off, he was much more appealing. So why did she lean against his shoulder and tip up her face? She couldn't resist. Now she had uncovered the painful, secret truth that prompted his bravado.

She flipped her gaze from Jack's eyes to the starry sky. "I…you…Jack…you're okay…more than okay…a smart, kind, good person." She almost told him how much she liked him, but she wanted to hear him say the words first. "You don't need to work so hard to impress everybody. I'm more impressed by what's on the inside."

"Thank you." Jack burned his gaze into her eyes. "I like you, Jill. You're honest and nice. A darn good teacher. And did I mention pretty?" He removed a mitt and ran a gentle finger under her cold chin.

Mesmerized by the starlight in his ocean eyes, she formed her mouth into a surprised O and relaxed it just in time to feel his lips brush hers in a delicious swirl of warm breath and cool breeze. Excitement and wonder squashed the air from her lungs and made her slightly dizzy. He liked her and valued her good qualities. Jack, of all people, thought she was pretty. He didn't mind her less-than-perfect body. Mr. Fitness accepted her, ample curves and all.

Could she really take a chance on a flawed, new man, especially an almost relative and confirmed coworker? The whole, surprising experience was almost too much to process. She moistened her tingling lips. She didn't regret the intimate moment for one second, but was she ready for the next step?

Chapter 14

A quip from Jack: Do you believe in love at first sight, or should I walk by again?

****

"I'm home." Jack announced his arrival back at Cody and Shauna's place a little louder than he intended. Vibrating with excitement, he shut the door with a clunk.

After his tender, surprise kiss on Jill's lips, Jack's heart still raced. In that breathtaking moment, certainty struck. Without a doubt, she was the missing piece of his puzzling life. He needed to meet her again outside of school—the sooner, the better.

Inside, the warm air rushed close, and he rubbed together his chilly hands. His son and daughter-in-law's small bungalow was a solid, starter home, decorated in trendy shades of gray, black, and beige. They poured most of their spare cash into Burger Town and never overextended their budget. Jack was proud of the way they worked as a team and planned for the future—skills he and Tina never modelled.

"Hi, Jack."

Shauna's voice croaked. Darn. He should show more consideration. For a young woman, she tired easily. While she waited for Cody to return from work, she often napped on the couch in a nest of matching toss cushions.

"How was your date with Mom?" She rolled to a sitting position and dragged a gray blanket over her shoulders.

Jack fell into a black armchair that only appeared comfortable and tapped his palms on the narrow arms. "Where should I start?" He grinned, leaned back, and extended his legs. He dug his cold toes into the black-and-white area rug, and they throbbed from being chilled and crammed into stiff skates.

Under the shadowy moonlight overhead and the white lights that illuminated the rink, Jill's pale, brown eyes had glinted almost gold. Her scent hinted of summer, his favorite season. Her low-key humor made him laugh. He liked her quiet, pleasant appearance. Less than two weeks ago, he never pictured himself attracted to a woman like no one he ever dated, but now he understood why things never worked out the way he hoped. The other women weren't really his type. They weren't Jill. "Let's just say your mom is one special lady." An electric charge tingled in Jack's chest.

"I agree. I couldn't ask for a better, more devoted mom." Shauna yawned and stretched. "But she could use a little more fun and action in her life."

"I noticed. And yours truly is ready for the challenge." He shifted and straightened. He didn't need to boast to impress Jill. She appreciated him, flaws and all.

"Go for it." Shauna hugged a pillow.

"Go for what?" With a rush of cold air, Cody arrived home and poked his head from the hallway into the living room doorway.

"Your dad thinks he can sweep Mom off her feet. Or should I say skates, Jack?"

"She showed me up tonight. I landed on my butt once, unlike Jill." Jack laughed and shook his head. He wasn't a superstar on ice, but nobody expected him to always do well, especially not Jill. She pointed out he didn't need to brag. "Yeah, I like her a lot."

"Hi, honey." Cody crossed the room, bent, and kissed Shauna. "Maybe soon you'll have a combined father-in-law and stepdad."

Shauna raised her eyebrows. "A package deal? Could be interesting to explain…"

"Two for the price of one. Highly efficient for family events." Jack chuckled and thrust out of the chair. The show of young love shot an arrow through his heart. Smart, lucky kids found the right one. When he married many years ago, he had high hopes, but he dragged along too much baggage to be the partner Tina needed. Maybe now, even at his age, he could discover true love…with a woman named Jill. "I'll leave you alone to canoodle. Good night." He raised a hand in a half wave and headed for his room to attend to important business.

In the spare room downstairs, his temporary home, he did an online search and paced around three sides of his bed. The space wasn't fancy, but it held everything he needed—a bed, dresser, chair, and even a small desk. A plaid, blue-and-gray duvet kept him plenty warm, and a few of Shauna's photos of old buildings around town added local color. She showed natural talent. Was Jill artistic, too?

He found the number he needed and glanced at his watch. If Merilee was still busy with tonight's tour and didn't answer, he'd leave a message. Anticipation darting up and down his spine, he called and listened to three, shrill rings.

"I'm sorry I can't take your call right now."

Sure enough, a recording of Merilee's singsong voice greeted him.

"If you'd like to book tickets for the Sweetheart Tour, please, leave a message, but first, what did the paper clip say to the magnet on Valentine's Day?" She giggled. "I find you very attractive. Well, ta-ta for now. I'll return your call soon."

Jack smiled at her over-the-top enthusiasm and waited for the beep. "Hello, Merilee. It's Jack Ryan. I had so much fun last time I'd like to reserve two spots for February fourteenth." He recited his phone number. "Have you heard this one? Why do tennis players avoid Valentine's Day? Because love means nothing."

He chuckled, clicked off the call, and pumped a fist. This time, the tour would be a legit date with a very special woman. As soon as Merilee confirmed the tickets, he'd invite Jill to join him for a romantic redo of the last tour. Within two weeks, everything had changed. He liked her. She liked him. What could possibly go wrong?

****

—Hey, Momsy. I hear you fell in love! ;)—

Jill smiled at the text message from Shauna, and her hands quivered around the phone. Setting it on her lap, she adjusted the brown, fleece blanket around her shoulders and tucked her toes underneath Georgia's furry side. Jack had a good time, too.

—Hardly. What did Jack say?—

Jill's lips still tingled from his magical kiss. He barely touched her, but his gentle presence and soft breath on her face awakened a blizzard of feelings.

From a spot on the living room sofa, she stared at the familiar lights on the houses across the street. She would always remember every detail of this evening.

—*He likes you!*—

The feeling was mutual, but how much should she tell her daughter? The whole arrangement—dating Shauna's father-in-law, who happened to live with her and Cody, and who worked at the same school—was complicated and a little close for comfort.

—*We had fun. I haven't skated in ages.*—

Jill took a deep breath and waited for Shauna's response.

—*How do you feel?*—

Trust Shauna to probe for details.

—*Like I should soon head to bed.*—

Jill wasn't ready to share her private excitement. She pretended to miss the intent of Shauna's question, but even if she tucked in, she wouldn't sleep. She leaned forward and stroked Georgia's soft back.

—*About Jack?*—

Shauna always persisted, even as a child. Clearly, tonight, she wouldn't give up until she learned more. Poising her thumbs, Jill considered how to reply.

—*He's funny and nice.*—

She'd allow Shauna a peek. She didn't add the truth that whirred in her heart. *He gives me hope I could love again. He makes me feel like an attractive woman. He trusted me with his secrets.* The snow on the window ledge framed the wintery scene outside. It was a perfect picture of the evening when everything brightened.

—*You like him. I knew it!*—

—*Have a good night, Shauna. xo*—

—Don't avoid the topic, Momsy. But ok. You, too. Sweet dreams (of Jack). LOL—

Still smiling, Jill tossed aside her phone. She hugged the blanket over her shoulders, leapt up, and spun. Wonder and joy twirled in her chest. She couldn't wait for school tomorrow and to say good morning to a certain gym teacher. Keeping her distance like she promised Nola might prove a challenge.

Chapter 15

A valentine joke from Goldview School announcements: What did the cucumber say to the pickle?

You mean a great dill to me.

****

The next morning at school, in the hallway outside her classroom, Jill jumped at the sensation of a warm hand on her lower back. She spun and faced Jack. "Not here. I told Nola I'd keep romance away from school." Her face grew warm. She'd stay serene on the outside and wouldn't show her insides tumbled like a load of laundry in a clothes dryer.

"Sorry. I couldn't resist." He stepped back.

She breathed the hallway smells of running shoes and cleaning solution and scanned Jack's freshly-shaven face, white T-shirt, and navy tracksuit. Dressed for the first gym class of the day, he stood trim and fit as ever. She slid her hand to the bottom of her thick, beige sweater but stopped before she tugged it lower over the hips of dark, brown pants. She needed to accept her shape now and not feel so self-conscious.

"I have a quick question. Would you like to join me on another Sweetheart Tour on February fourteenth?" He glanced over his shoulder. "It would be a real date. Not like last time."

His blue eyes beamed bright, and his expression

was as expectant as a boy asking a parent for a new soccer ball. The morning bell jangled, and soon kids would swarm the hallways. She didn't have much time to think over his invitation, but she didn't need it. On this tour, with a new man by her side, she would belong. "I'd love to." She smiled at the way he puffed his chest. He believed she liked the true, inner him.

"Great because I already bought the tickets." He heaved a breath and grinned.

Jill laughed. "What if I declined?" She felt as sunshiny as the artwork on the wall behind Jack.

"I didn't have a plan B." He shrugged.

"Then today's your lucky day. At the sound of footsteps padding along the hallway and a chorus of voices, she backed away. "Thank you." She smiled and, shocking herself, blew a quick kiss. "See you later."

"You bet." He widened his eyes and swivelled toward the gym door.

Cheeks burning hot, how would Jill concentrate on class now?

Her students hustled toward the classroom and stirred a draft of cold, outside air that clung to their jackets.

Shivering, she hugged her arms around her middle. "Good morning, James. Good morning, Caleb." She smiled at the identical twins. They were two of the mischief makers—possibly even bullies—who egged on other kids to taunt poor Oscar. She rattled off names and nodded at the boys and girls. Later this week, she'd meet with the twins' parents and Oscar's mom to gain their support to end the unacceptable behavior.

As she supervised the kids hanging jackets and settling at their desks, she pictured herself on

Valentine's Day, riding the tour bus and then dining with Jack. She'd wear her new, pink sweater—an unusual color in her wardrobe but perfect for the occasion—with white beadwork around the neckline. Sparkly, pink earrings and dressy, black pants would complete the ensemble. She'd apply a touch of mascara to accentuate her eyes and sweep gloss over her lips. Jack would gaze across the table at dinner like he couldn't wait to kiss her in a long, slow caress. Longing flipped in her stomach, and she dragged back her focus to the morning's agenda.

For the next three days, careful to act like nothing more than a coworker, Jill joined Jack at lunchtime for brisk walks around the school neighborhood. Although tempted, she begged off evening dates so she could get a hair trim and mark assignments. At noon hour, the cold air cleared her head, and the exercise boosted her energy. In his presence, she tingled with excitement. Building on the bond she shared with Jack as an in-law—or his label, an outlaw—she accepted him like an old friend she had trusted forever.

Traipsing along, puffing wisps of white, she confided how, for several years, loneliness and a sense of failure had stolen her drive and cocooned her at home. "Food comforted me, but now I'm determined to change. The Sweetheart Tour inspired me to quit procrastinating."

"Congrats. Exercise helps everything." Jack swung his arms and laughed. "I follow that theory, anyway."

Jill groaned and laughed. "I know. I know. You sound like a recording." She picked up her pace. The schoolyard stretched ahead in a fluffy, white blanket tromped with footprints. It glittered in the sunlight like sequins that matched her bright outlook.

"Can I tell you something?" Boots clumping, Jack strode along a snowy sidewalk.

"Sure." Jill admired his even profile and pink cheekbones and followed his gaze to a row of houses in a neat, colorful line facing the school. "Go ahead."

"You're very attractive, Jill. I admire your pretty face and full figure." He cleared his throat and glanced over. "And you're full of wisdom and strength and fun. You don't need to adjust your sweater over your stomach, or hips, or whatever you try to cover."

Jill's mouth dried, and she swallowed. She absorbed the honk of a car horn and the crunch of their footsteps on packed snow. He noticed she wasn't perfect, and he didn't care. He didn't want her to hide her body. She was just fine. "Thank you, Jack. You're very kind." He accepted her—flaws and all.

Wait until Shauna and Audrey heard everything was just about perfect…or was it?

****

After lunch on Thursday, Jack passed a youngish, plump woman who shuffled toward the door. With the same moon face and straggly hair, she must be Oscar's mother. "How did the meeting go?" He stuck his head into the doorway of Jill's classroom.

Jill glanced up and smiled. Holding a fistful of colored markers, she strolled to greet him.

With her hair bouncing in loose curls, she looked youthful and carefree. "Was Oscar's mom aware of his struggles?" He met Jill's gaze and resisted a second glance at her curvaceous body in a flannel, cream shirt and brown, denim jeans.

"She knows but has no idea how to build his

112

confidence." Twisting both hands around the markers, Jill shook her head. "We brainstormed options."

"First on the list should be to set a good example." Jack crossed his arms over his chest. Anybody could choose a healthier lifestyle. If the kid didn't lug so much extra weight, he wouldn't be such an easy target.

"What do you mean?" Jill narrowed her eyes.

"I passed his chunky mom in the hallway. She's a serious butterball. If she ate better and exercised, she'd help Oscar shape up and feel better. I know. Lardy is not cool."

Jill opened and closed her mouth.

Her face paled and then flushed the color of the pink, felt pen in her hands. With her lips pressed into a firm, straight line, she resembled an old-fashioned teacher about to inflict detention. He swallowed.

"Thank you for your input." She spun and stalked to her desk. "I need to get ready for afternoon classes." She paused. "Jack, you better find someone else to take my place on the tour."

"But Jill…"

"I just realized this relationship won't work." She stared at the papers on her desk.

Jack's confidence plummeted to the floor, and he slouched away like she shoved him out of the room. He wanted to help, but obviously, he made a terrible mistake. Sure, his words rang harsh, but why did his candid comments about Oscar's mom offend Jill to such an extreme, and how could he make amends?

Chapter 16

Advice from Audrey: Nobody is perfect. That's why pencils have erasers.

*****

Jill curled her feet underneath her in a chair next to Audrey's fireplace. After the painful exchange with Jack at school today, she needed advice. "I won't stay long. Shauna invited me to go to their place around eight. She insisted the visit couldn't wait." She bowed her head and moaned. "But if I go, I can't avoid Jack."

Panting in the heat, Georgia sprawled nearby on a patterned area rug.

Jill often escaped to the calming refuge at Audrey's place, but so far, she felt no better. Usually so comforting, the quiet, jazz music and earth-tone furnishings did little to soothe her heavy disappointment. Of course, the crystal hearts shimmering in the window, a heart-shaped dish of cinnamon hearts, and the pink bouquet on the coffee table didn't help. The tasteful, Valentine's décor only emphasized the sorry state of Jill's heart. Even Audrey's sympathetic expression behind her tortoiseshell glasses and her murmured reassurance didn't diminish Jill's pain one bit.

"Tell me more." In the chair on the other side of the fire, Audrey tipped her head and blinked.

Sipping honey-lemon tea, Jill cradled the mug and

let the warmth seep into her hands. "I thought Jack was deeper and kinder than he first appears. Well, I was wrong."

"What happened to change your mind? Audrey sipped her tea.

"Jack pretended he liked my curves. I believed he appreciated the inner and the outer me…just the way I am…extra pounds and all." She patted a thigh, and her words caught in her throat. With more activity, her shape might change, but she exercised to feel better and not because Jack approved. "Now I know the truth. Mr. Fitness doesn't respect a person who struggles with weight."

"I have no doubt he likes you—a lot. Everybody on the tour noticed the way he admired you. We all sensed the chemistry." Audrey leaned forward.

Jill set down her mug on a nearby table and studied her hands. "His comments about Oscar's mom were insensitive, and I couldn't help but take them personally. She isn't much bigger than me." Her throat tightened. "He shouldn't judge." With Jack's personal history, he should know better.

"I understand." Audrey listened and nodded. "Does he know why you're so upset?"

Jill shook her head. "Right after school, I hurried home." She inhaled the fragrant steam wafting close.

"Talk with him, Jill." Audrey placed a firm hand on the arm of her chair. "Nobody's perfect. Everyone has flaws." She laughed and scrunched her face. "Even teachers still have things to learn."

"But…"

Audrey grinned and covered her ears. "I won't listen to arguments." She dropped her hands. "At least, share your feelings. He's probably hurt and confused."

Jill stared at the licking flames. Could she explain to Jack why his comments cut like a nasty putdown? Could she forgive his blunder and move forward? Would she ever fully accept her less-than-perfect figure? She pictured the cozy bus trip, the delicious, gourmet dinner, and the chance to hold hands and even kiss in the dark. The pain in her heart eased and intensified at the same time.

Jill glanced at her watch. "Oops, two minutes past eight means I'm late. I'll think about your advice. Thank you, big sis. I owe you—again." She smiled at Audrey, tipped out of her chair, and hugged her.

Georgia circled and thwacked her tail against Jill's legs.

Jill zipped her jacket and was about to leave the warmth of Audrey's home when she retrieved her phone from a pocket and scanned a series of text messages.

—*Momsy, did somebody die?*—

—*What happened at school? Jack's shoulders sag to his elbows. Right after dinner, he bolted downstairs to his room.*—

—*Are you on your way over?*—

—*Mom?*—

—*Where are you? We're waiting.*—

Reading the string of messages from Shauna, Jill bit her bottom lip to control a quiver.

—*Just leaving Audrey's. See you soon.*—

"Shauna's worried about Jack." Jill grimaced at Audrey. "She asked why he's depressed."

"She feels sorry for the poor guy." Audrey squatted and petted Georgia. "But you can fix things. Romance is good for the soul." She stood and rubbed Jill's arm. "C'mon, little sis. Don't trip over your frown. Good luck."

Gulping air, Jill jogged to Shauna and Cody's place. Crunching snow with every stride, she hunched her shoulders against the cold. She hurried by neat, modest homes with welcoming lights and tidy sidewalks.

Even if difficult, she'd follow Audrey's advice and communicate with Jack. He needed to understand the issue, and she needed to be respected.

Scooping mouthfuls of snow, Georgia romped along.

Life was so simple for a dog. Puffing hard, Jill paused on the front steps before she rang the bell. When she faced Jack, she had no idea how she'd react.

****

Jack rolled off his bed and glanced in the round mirror above the dresser. He ran fingers through his hair and straightened his gray sweatshirt. Shauna had reminded him he should join her and Cody in the living room at eight. Trepidation jabbed his stomach. Jill was invited, too.

Climbing the steps to the main level, he replayed their conversation for the hundredth time. She disapproved of his comments about Oscar's mom. Sure, he used strong language. After suffering his share of ridicule, he should know better, but tactful was not his middle name. He trusted he didn't need to edit his words around Jill. She believed he wanted the best for Oscar, so why the strong reaction in defense of the boy's mother? His head ached from confusion and regret. Never mind the expense of the tour tickets. Now, her seat would be empty.

"I hope you invited me because Cody baked an apple pie." Jack sniffed the air and detected the scent of pastry and cinnamon. Hardly hungry, he forced a chuckle and plunked into a gray chair that was almost the same shade as his shirt and drummed the arms with his fingers. He scanned the gray, black, and beige color scheme and landed his gaze on a vase of red roses. They were probably a surprise gift from Cody to Shauna. The symbol of love burned, and he closed his eyes in a long, slow blink. Opening them, he focused on a black toss cushion that better suited his mood.

"I'll be right there, Dad," Cody called from the kitchen.

"Here's Mom." Shauna swung open the front door.

Jack gripped the arms of the chair and stared at the entranceway. Dressed in cozy, olive-green loungewear, Shauna radiated more energy than usual.

Georgia bounded in first and headed straight for Jack.

"Hey, pup." Jack rubbed her head and neck. At least, Jill's dog liked him." A cool draft jetted across the room and carried the smell of clean, outside air. Any second, Jill would appear.

"I'll take your jacket, Momsy. Come in." Shauna held out a hand.

"Hello, Jack." Jill rounded the corner and raised a hand in a small wave. She glanced around the room and chose the far end of the sofa, the farthest seat away.

"Hi, Jill. Long time, no see." His heart thumped an intense beat. He wanted to touch her pink cheeks and tousled hair. Even without a smile, she was attractive in an intriguing, subtle way. He imagined her voluptuous figure in his arms and swallowed. Sitting still in her company would not be easy. He fought the urge to leap out of his chair and pace. Why did he agree to torture himself at a family visit?

Chapter 17

Advice Jill gave Shauna: "Don't marry someone you can live with; marry someone you can't live without."

Jack's advice to Cody: Happy wife, happy life.

****

Nestled into the corner of the beige, leather sofa, Jill folded her arms over her chest. The aroma of Cody's fresh-baked apple pie didn't tempt her as usual. "Lie down, Georgia." Snapping a finger, she pointed at the floor. She forced a half smile but couldn't think of a thing to say to the humans in the room.

"I can't wait until after dessert." Shauna perched on the edge of a gray chair near Jack. She smiled and swept her gaze from Jack to Jill.

Shifting, Cody leaned on the doorjamb by the opening to the kitchen.

For the first time, Jill spotted two gifts stacked next to Shauna's feet. Was it Jack's birthday? Were they here to celebrate? She hardly felt in the mood for a party.

Shauna leapt up, grabbed the gifts, and handed one to Jack and one to Jill.

"What? Why?" Jill admired the silver paper tied with a pink ribbon. Across the room, Jack held an identical parcel, except for its blue ribbon. Could the colors possibly hint of what she hoped? Sudden excitement fizzed like soda in her chest.

"Open them at the same time." Shauna clapped together her hands.

Jill slipped off the ribbon and tore open the parcel. Lifting the lid, she held her breath and held up a pink T-shirt emblazoned with *World's Best Grandma*.

At the same time, Jack unveiled a blue T-shirt labelled *World's Best Grandpa*.

"You're having a baby!" Jill shrieked and, still clutching the shirt, jumped and hugged Shauna and then Cody.

"Not just one..." Cody draped an arm around Shauna's waist.

"Double trouble?" Jack pumped a fist, joined the circle, and hugged Cody and Shauna.

"Twins!" Shauna thrust both arms above her head. "A boy and a girl."

"How wonderful!" Jill dropped open her mouth and flung trembling hands over her cheeks. She had dreamed of the day she'd become a grandma, and she couldn't imagine better news. No wonder Shauna looked so pale and tired these days. Pregnant with not one but two babies explained everything.

Overcome with emotion, Jill almost hugged Jack, then stiffened and backed away. She wouldn't let the celebration muddle her feelings any more than they were already. No doubt, Jack shared her excitement, and he'd embrace the role of grandpa, but he might not be the considerate guy she needed. Butterflies flitted around the joy in her stomach. She wouldn't avoid the conflict altogether, but she'd deal with Jack another day. Tonight she'd focus on the most important thing— two beautiful additions to the family.

An hour later, Shauna smothered a yawn and gathered plates. "I'll be right back to say goodbye." She shuffled in fluffy, white slippers.

"Let me help." Cody followed her to the kitchen.

The clatter of dishes and murmured conversation meandered into the living room. "I better let the mama-to-be get to bed." Left alone with Jack, Jill jumped up to make a quick escape. She refused to let tension spoil Shauna and Cody's good news. Tilting to pet Georgia, she avoided eye contact with Jack. Her throat squeezed at the way, in an unguarded moment, his expression and shoulders drooped. Could a relationship possibly feel right ever again?

****

"Please, join me for breakfast tomorrow morning." Jack scooted forward, his thighs hardening into two planks of wood. He rubbed them, but they didn't relax. From the kitchen, water trickled in the sink. He needed to hurry before Cody and Shauna returned to say goodnight.

Preparing to leave, Jill paused in the middle of the room and flicked her gaze along the sofa and over the area rug to Jack.

"We need to talk. I'm sorry I messed up. I'd like to understand…" His expression felt crumpled and heavy. Apparently, he had a lot to learn from Jill. How could he fix his blunder? "Meet me for breakfast tomorrow. Please, say yes."

Crossing her arms, she shook her head. "Sorry. Not tomorrow. A school morning would be too rushed." She folded her lips into a thin line.

"Then how about Saturday?"

She sighed. "I guess so."

"Thank you, Jill." Relief rushed from his chest to his fingertips. He gripped the arms of his chair. "I promise you won't be sorry."

Blinking, she glanced away.

Her eyes shone brighter than usual. Did they glisten with tears? He cleared his throat and wracked his brain for words to lighten the mood. "You look young for a grandma."

"Thank you, but looks aren't everything." She spun and marched toward the kitchen.

Jack sighed and hung his head. Did he just blow it again?

****

At nine o'clock Saturday morning, Jack peered at Jill over a table at Burger Town. A dozen red roses displayed in a clear vase decorated the space beside the napkin holder. Shauna had insisted he couldn't go wrong with flowers to show how much he cared.

"They're beautiful." Smiling, Jill glanced over. "Thank you, again."

Cody ran a busy diner, and even this early, most of the orange booths were filled with customers. The homey place hummed with muted conversations, servers' footsteps, and clattering dishes. The aroma of bacon, eggs, and toast wafted from the kitchen, and Jack gulped steaming, bitter coffee. He breathed warm, humid air and inhaled a whiff of his ham and cheese omelette.

Jill picked at a bowl of sliced fruit topped with yogurt and granola.

The scents of strawberries and vanilla mingled with his hearty breakfast. Her bronze-colored sweater shaded her eyes the color of toffee, but they didn't show their usual sheen. "Tell me your concerns. I offended you, and I'm sorry. I shouldn't have dissed Oscar's mom. Sometimes my big mouth gets me in trouble. But I just really want to help the kid."

"From the day you arrived at Goldview School, you've supported Oscar. He's really excited you asked him to keep stats at volleyball games." Jill swirled a blackberry around her dish. She glanced up. "But you're right. What you said about his mom was...offensive...and hurtful."

"True. I made a mistake." He stabbed a bite of egg and chewed. He couldn't argue, but why did Jill care so much? "I shouldn't have judged her." He squirmed under Jill's hard scrutiny.

"You deserve credit for how you changed your eating and exercise habits. You're a rock star, unlike most people. But don't forget the other side—when you were ashamed of your size. Oscar's mom might be overweight and out of shape, but..." Jill stared past Jack's shoulder.

Her eyes glossed, and he wanted to hug her.

"But she's not much different than me." She hurried through her words. "I'm not exactly model thin. If you criticize her, you might as well lump me in the same category."

Jack dropped his fork, raised a palm, and thunked the side of his head. "Jill, I'm an idiot. An inconsiderate, *sorry* idiot. I admire everything about you. You attract me like no other. Please, forgive me." He searched her face for any sign of softening.

"Not yet." She blinked, sipped coffee, and sighed. "I need to know why you were so harsh. You should understand better than anyone a person isn't defined by appearance." She stirred her yogurt.

Her eyes burned with disapproval, and he wanted to grab the menu propped at the end of the table and shield his face. She raised a good question. Why? He studied the cantaloupe slice on the edge of his place. Shaped like a smile, it grinned at his misery. "I'm proud of the changes I made." He shook his head. "If I can do it, anybody can." Did he think he was superior now? "I labelled her the same way, after years of ridicule, I judged myself. I viewed us as part of the same, sad club."

Jill fidgeted with the neckline of her sweater.

Now did she understand? "Maybe..." Thick air, laden with the smells of toast, hashbrowns, and coffee, smothered his breath. The clink of utensils intensified, beat into his brain, and jostled free his secret. "Maybe I felt safer playing on offense...with jokes, cracks, and even insults. Stuck on defense was...is...tough."

Jill raised a napkin to her lips and nodded.

"But now I see I was wrong...way off base...a bit of a jerk. What more can I say? I'm sorry and will do better in the future." He clenched his knife and fork. Did she believe his promise?

****

"Don't just tell me. Show me." Jill twisted a napkin on her lap and searched his somber expression. Her entire body ached. Underneath her baby joy, she floundered—crushed by hurtful comments, sleepless nights, and the longest day of teaching she ever endured. Could he live up to her expectations? Would her heart heal?

With furrowed brow, Jack looked as earnest as a teen learning to drive. His denim shirt accentuated the blue of his eyes. *Stay strong, Jill. Remain firm.* No matter how much she lectured, waves of compassion— and desire?—rippled through her chest.

"Absolutely." He nodded, exhaled, and sank deeper into his seat. Underneath him, the orange, leatherette covering squeaked.

"Sometimes, you might need to bite your tongue. Mom used to say, 'If you can't say anything nice, don't—'"

"Don't say anything at all." He chuckled and rubbed the back of his neck. "I heard the same advice from my mom."

"I accept your apology, but…" Jill cupped her coffee mug and leaned forward.

"Not a *but*." He tipped back his head and groaned.

At his exaggerated dismay, she allowed a half smile. "Promise you will never judge a person's size— including mine. If I eat dessert, I don't want to feel guilty or shamed. You can't say a word." She clunked her mug onto the table. "Be yourself, but be kind."

"I promise." He grinned and raised a palm. "Scout's honor."

"Thank you." Her burning misery eased, and hope leapt in her heart. "I believe in you." She dipped her spoon and chewed a mouthful of fruit and granola. "Oh, and one more thing…"

"Yes?" Jack lifted his eyebrows.

"Occasional flowers are always a nice touch." Smiling, she leaned across the table and stroked his forearm.

"I'll keep that tip in mind." Jack laughed and straightened his shoulders.

"Definitely, you're off to a good start." She

glanced from Jack to the bouquet. "And don't worry." She tilted her head. "My wish won't break the bank. These red roses are gorgeous, but I like pink carnations just as much."

****

Unburdened, Jack grinned and admired Jill's softened expression. The way her face shone, she should wear that bronze sweater more often. Or were relief and happiness the real reasons for her glow? His heart pumped double time as if he ran a marathon or hit a hole-in-one. She liked and trusted him, and he wouldn't let her down. Now, the weight of his stupidity lifted and mingled with the smells of breakfast and the buzz of customers. Life beamed much brighter. "I can't wait to be a grandpa. We'll have so much fun with those twins. What about you, Grandma?" He swallowed the last bite of bacon and wiped a napkin over his mouth.

"I'm thrilled, but I'm not *your* grandma." She widened her eyes.

"Right. Sorry, *Jill*." He quirked an eyebrow. "Hey, you *will* be my date on the Sweetheart Tour, won't you?"

"Hmmm. Let me think." She crossed her arms over her heart. "Okay, I accept."

"If we weren't in public, I might kiss you right now." He stretched over the table and squeezed her hands.

"If we weren't in public, I might like that idea very much." She covered her cheeks.

He glanced at his watch. "I better let you start errands." Desire spun in his chest like a tether ball. Now he could count down the minutes to their

Valentine's Day date and discover where the bus ride would lead.

Chapter 18

Jack's valentine card to Jill: "I know it's cheesy, but we were meant to brie together."

Jill's valentine card to Jack: "In the hot chocolate of my life, you are the marshmallow."

****

"I'm excited about our evening." Jill snuggled next to Jack near the back of the Sweetheart Tour bus. She breathed his subtle scent, as fresh and irresistible as a beach on a sunny day. The weather was frosty, and the interior was chilly, but her heart was warm. Murmured conversation buzzed down the aisle, and the windows radiated cold air, yet nothing mattered except the man at her side. Tonight held the promise of a true, romantic date.

"Me, too, my valentine." Jack brushed a finger under her chin.

Anticipation fluttered from her stomach to her chest. After her serious talk with Jack and his genuine apology, she had floated through the rest of the weekend secure in the knowledge he committed to change. If he slipped up, he'd repair the damage and start again. Jill's new exercise regime didn't show yet on the outside, but inside, she felt lighter than ever. With an attractive man beside her and twin grandbabies on the way, she brimmed with more joy than a child on Christmas morning.

"Good evening, lovebirds." Merilee singsonged into the mic at the front of the bus.

She bounced and sparkled in a pink outfit the color of bubblegum. Perfect for her hosting role, her love of fun and adventure was contagious. Even if Jill's new, active lifestyle prompted a fraction of Merilee's vivacious energy, she'd celebrate.

"You are about to embark on a lovely evening of fine food and even finer romance. Our handsome driver, Ross—who also happens to be my sweetie pie—and I both thank you for being our guests."

Jack's warm hand closed around hers, and the heat travelled up her arm straight to her heart. Two weeks ago, she had dreaded the tour, and tonight she anticipated every moment. Before long, she and Jack would be co-grandparents, and who knew where their relationship might lead? As the bus rolled onto a country, gravel road, the motion jostled her against Jack, and the sensation burned through her jacket to her shoulder. How could a simple touch ignite such an intense flame?

"Before I switch on a selection of dreamy love songs, I want to share some very exciting news." Merilee's beaming face shone through the dim lighting. "Ross and I shared a special Valentine's Day lunch earlier today, and guess what? He proposed! Of course, I said yes." She raised her left hand and flashed a glittering, diamond ring. "I met my sweetie on the Christmas Cookie Tour, and now, I'm engaged to the man of my dreams. I'm over the moon."

Merilee's lilting, joyful voice crackled through the speakers, and Jill joined the passengers' applause. How exciting and romantic for Merilee and Ross! If they rediscovered love at their age, maybe she could, too.

"We'll get married this summer." Merilee threw a hand over her chest and then leaned over and kissed Ross's cheek. "Oops. I better not distract our handsome driver." Giggling, she scanned the group. "Sit back, and enjoy the ride. Love is in the air."

"Maybe we'll be as lucky as Ross and Merilee." Jack squeezed her hand.

"I hope so." Heart melting, Jill tipped back her head and tingled at his delicious, magical kiss.

Epilogue

A month later, holding hands in sunshine bright enough to melt snowbanks, Jill and Jack scanned a yellow poster in the window of Omar's Foods.

Hop to it!
Merilee's Easter Bunny Bash
Brunch...Easter eggs...Games...
Nonstop fun for all ages.
April 5-20 Book now!
1-800-FUN-TOUR merilee@funtour.com

"Be my date?" Jack squeezed her hand.

"Always." Jill giggled and tipped up her face for a sweet kiss. "Next year, we can bring our twin grandbabies."

A word about the author...

Margot Johnson writes feel-good stories of dreams, family, and romance. She is the author of two novels and two novellas.

Before turning her focus to the fun, writing life, Margot held leadership roles in human resources and communications. She lives in the Canadian prairies with her husband and golden retriever.

Get in touch with Margot Johnson on social media:

Website: margotjohnson.ca
Facebook: MargotJohnsonAuthor
Twitter: @AuthorMargot

Other Titles by this Author
Let it Snowball, book 1,Merilee Tours
Love Leads the Way
Love Takes Flight

Thank you for purchasing
this publication of The Wild Rose Press, Inc.

For questions or more information
contact us at
info@thewildrosepress.com.

The Wild Rose Press, Inc.
www.thewildrosepress.com

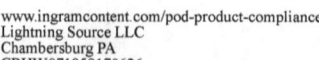